MW01673707

Undertones

SALZWASSER
VERLAG

Robert Buchanan

Undertones

Reprint of the original, first published in 1863.

1st Edition 2022 | ISBN: 978-3-37500-450-7

Verlag (Publisher): Salzwasser Verlag GmbH, Zeilweg 44, 60439 Frankfurt, Deutschland
Vertretungsberechtigt (Authorized to represent): E. Roepke, Zeilweg 44, 60439 Frankfurt, Deutschland
Druck (Print): Books on Demand GmbH, In de Tarpen 42, 22848 Norderstedt, Deutschland

UNDERTONES.

BY

ROBERT BUCHANAN.

"Shades, that hang
Upon the region whither we are bound."

THE EXCURSION.

"Cœlum ipsum petimus."

HORACE.

LONDON:

1863.

DEDICATION.

TO

JOHN WESTLAND MARSTON, ESQ., LL.D.,

Author of the "Patrician's Daughter," "A Lady in Her Own Right," &c

DEAR WESTLAND MARSTON,

To whom can I more appropriately dedicate these *Undertones* than to the man whose friendship has been a comfort to me during four years of the bitterest struggle and disappointment, and whose voice has whispered "courage" when I seemed faltering down the easy descent to Acheron? The world knows least of your noble soul. High-minded, gracious-hearted, possessed of the true instinct of an artist, you have laid me under a debt of affection which I can never repay; yet take the Book, as a token that I love and honour you.

Ever yours,

ROBERT BUCHANAN.

LONDON, *November 1st*, 1863.

PREFACE.

It is difficult for the uninitiated to understand or sympathise with the difficulties which have attended the composition of these *Undertones;* yet the class of mind to whom the book appeals will comprehend the statement that the author has been compelled, at too early an age, to get his bread by letters. Faults may be found with certain liberties taken with old theories, certain tentative interpretations of ambiguous myths; but no fault should be found with the author's assertion that the mere completion of his ambitious design —no matter how faulty the workmanship may be— is, under the circumstances, a triumph in itself and an earnest of better things.

CONTENTS

*** One or two of the shorter pieces have been printed before in the *Athenæum.*

PROLOGUE.

TO DAVID IN HEAVEN.

"*Quo diversus abis?*"

"*Quem Di diligunt, adolescens moritur.*"

TO DAVID IN HEAVEN.

1.

Lo! the slow moon foaming
Thro' fleecy mists of gloaming,
Furrowing with pearly front the jewel-powder'd sky!
Lo, the bridge moss-laden,
Arch'd like foot of maiden,
And on the bridge, in silence, looking upward, you and I!
Lo, the pleasant season
Of reaping and of mowing—
The foam-fringed moon above,—beneath, the river dusky flowing!

2.

Violet-colour'd shadows,
Blown from scented meadows,
Float o'er us to the pine-wood dark from yonder blue corn-ridge;

The little river gushes
Thro' shady sedge and rushes,
And gray gnats murmur o'er the pools, beneath the mossy bridge ;—
And you and I stand darkly,
O'er the keystone leaning,
And watch the pale mesmeric moon, in the time of gleaners and gleaning.

3.

Do I dream, I wonder?
As, sitting sadly under
A lonely roof in London, thro' the grim square pane I gaze?
Here of thee I ponder,
In a dream, and yonder
The pale streets seem to stir and breathe beneath the white moon's rays.
By the vision cherish'd,
By the dark hope bravéd,
Do I but dream a hopeless dream, in the city that slew you, David?

4.

Is it fancy also,
That the light which falls so
Faintly upon the stony street below me as I write,
Near tall mountains passes
Thro' churchyard weeds and grasses,
Barely a mower's mile away from that small bridge, to-night?
And, where you are lying,—
Grass and flowers above you—
Is mingled with your sleeping face, as calm as the hearts that love you?

5.

Poet gentle-hearted,
Are you then departed,
And have you ceased to dream the dream we loved of old so well?
Has the deeply-cherish'd
Aspiration perish'd,
And are you happy, David, in that heaven where you dwell?

Have you found the secret
We, so wildly, sought for,
Is your young soul enswathed, at last, in the singing robes you fought for?

6.

In some heaven star-lighted,
Are you now united
Unto the poet-spirits that you loved, of English race?
Is Chatterton still dreaming?
And, to give it stately seeming,
Has the music of his last strong song passed into Keats's face?
Is Wordsworth there? and Spenser?
Beyond the grave's black portals,
Can the grand eye of Milton *see* the glory he sang to mortals?

7.

You at least could teach me,
Could your low voice reach me,
Where I sit and copy out for men my soul's strange speech,

Whether it be bootless,
Profitless, and fruitless,—
The weary aching upward strife to heights we cannot reach,
The fame we seek in sorrow,
The agony we forego not,
The haunting singing sense that makes us climb—whither we know not.

8.

Must it last for ever,
The passionate endeavour,
Ay, have you, there in heaven, hearts to throb and still aspire?
In the life you know now,
Render'd white as snow now,
Do fresher glory-heights arise, and beckon higher—higher?
Are you dreaming, dreaming,
Is your soul still roaming,
Still gazing upward as we gazed, of old in the autumn gloaming?

9.

Lo, the book I hold here,
In the city cold here!
I hold it with a gentle hand and love it as I may;
Lo, the weary moments!
Lo, the icy comments!
And lo, pale Fortune's knife of gold swift-lifted up to slay!
Has the strife no ending?
Has the song no meaning?
Linger I, idle as of old, while men are reaping or gleaning?

10.

Upward my face I turn to you,
I long for you, I yearn to you,
The pallid moonlight trances me to utt'rance wild and weak;
It is not that I mourn you,
To mourn you were to scorn you,
For you are one step nearer to the beauty singers seek.

But I want, and cannot see you,
I seek and cannot find you,
And, see! I touch the book of songs you tenderly left
behind you!

11.

Ay me! I bend above it,
With tearful eyes, and love it,
With gentle hand I touch the leaves, but cannot find
you there!
Mine eyes are haunted only
By that gloaming sweetly lonely,
The shadows on the mossy bridge, the glamour in the
air!
I touch the leaves, and only
See the glory they retain not—
The moon that is a lamp to Hope, who glorifies what
we gain not!

12.

The aching and the yearning,
The hollow undiscerning,

Uplooking want I still retain, darken the leaves I
touch—
Pale promise, with sad sweetness
Solemnizing incompleteness,
But ah, you knew so little then—and now you know
so much!
By the vision cherish'd
By the dark hope bravéd,
Have you, in heaven, shamed the song, by a loftier
music, David?

13.

I, who loved and knew you,
In the city that slew you,
Still hunger on, and thirst, and climb, proud-hearted
and alone.
Serpent-fears enfold me,
Syren-visions hold me,
And, like a wave, I gather strength, and gathering
strength, I moan;
Ay, the pale moon beckons,
Still I follow, aching,

And gather strength, only to make a louder moan,
in breaking!

14.

Tho' the world could turn from you,
This, at least, I learn from you:
Beauty and Truth, tho' never found, are worthy to be
sought,
The singer, upward-springing,
Is grander than his singing,
And tranquil self-sufficing joy illumes the dark of
thought.
This, at least, you teach me,
In a revelation:
That gods still snatch, as worthy death, the soul in its
aspiration.

15.

And I think, as you thought,
Poesy and Truth ought
Never to lie silent in the singer's heart on earth;
Tho' they be discarded,

Slighted, unrewarded,—
Tho', unto vulgar seeming, they appear of little worth,—
Yet tender brother-singers,
Young or not yet born to us,
May seek there, for the singer's sake, that love which sweeteneth scorn to us!

16.

While I sit in silence,
Comes from mile on mile hence,
From English Keats's Roman grave, a voice that sweetens toil!
Think you, no fond creatures
Drew comfort from the features
Of Chatterton, pale Phäethon, hurled down to sunless soil,
Scorch'd with sunlight lying,
Eyes of sunlight hollow,
But, see! upon the lips a gleam of the chrism of Apollo!

17.

Noble thought produces
Noble ends and uses,

Noble hopes are part of Hope wherever she may be,
Noble thought enhances
Life and all its chances,
And noble self is noble song,—all this I learn from thee!
And I learn, moreover,
Mid the city's strife too,
That such pure song as sweetens Death can sweeten the singer's life too!

18.

Lo, my Book!—I hold it
In weary hands, and fold it
Unto my heart, if only as a token I aspire;
And, by song's assistance,
Unto your dim distance,
My soul uplifted is on wings, and beckon'd higher, nigher.
By the higher wisdom
You return unspeaking,
Though endless, hopeless, be the search, we exalt our souls in seeking.

19.

But ah, that pale moon foaming
Thro' fleecy mists of gloaming,
Furrowing with pearly front the jewel-powder'd sky,
And ah, the days departed
With your friendship gentle-hearted,
And ah, the dream we dreamt that night, together, you and I!
Is it fashion'd wisely,
To help us or to blind us,
That at each height we gain we turn, and behold a heaven behind us?

THE UNDERTONES.

O Fame, thou haunting upward-urging hope,
That makest of the pale aspiring soul
A statue of Narcissus, still and fair
For evermore, and bending evermore
Over its beauteous image mirrorëd
In the swift current of our human life,
Eternally in act to clasp and kiss!
O Fame, teach thou this soul of mine to love
Some beauteous counterpart, and while it bends
Tremulously gazing on the image, blow
Thy trump aloud, and freeze it into stone!

THE UNDERTONES.

I.

ADES, KING OF HELL.

Orb'd in a rayless realm, alone,
Under the realm of sun and shower,
A palpable god with godlike power,
I, Ades, dwelt upon a throne.
Much darkness did my eyelids tire;
But thro' my veins the hid Sun's fire
Communicated impulse, hope, thought, passion, and desire.

2.

Beneath the caves where sunless loam
Grows dim and reddens into gold;
'Neath the fat earth-seams, where the cold
Rains thicken to the flowery foam
Fringing blue streams in summer zones;
Beneath the spheres where dead men's bones
Change darkly thro' slow centuries to marl and glittering stones.

3.

Eternities of lonely reign,
Full of faint dreams of day and night
And the white glamour of starry light,
Oppress'd my patience into pain;
Upward I sent a voice of prayer
That made black thunder in the air:
And "Ades craves a queen, O Zeus!" shook heaven unaware.

4.

The gods stopt short in full carouse,
And listen'd. On the streams of Hell
The whole effulgent conclave fell
As in a glass. With soft-arch'd brows,
And wings of dewy-tinctured dye,
Moist Iris listen'd blushingly;
And Heré sought the soul of Zeus with coldly eager
eye.

5.

Then the clear hyaline grew cold
And dim before the Father's face;
Gray meditation clothed the place;
And rising up Zeus cried, "Behold!"—
And on Olumpos' crystal wall
A kingly phantom cloudy and tall,
Throned, sceptred, crown'd, was darkly apparition'd at
the call.

6.

"Behold him—Dis!" the Father cried,
And the voice shook my throne forlorn:
Pale Hermes curl'd his lips in scorn,
And Iris drew her bow aside;
Artemis paled and did not speak;
Sheer fear flush'd Aphroditê's cheek;
And only owl-eyed Pallas look'd with pitying smile and meek.

7.

A weary night thro' earth and air
The shadow of my longing spread,
And not a goddess answerëd.
All nature darken'd at my prayer;
Which darkness earth and air did shroud,
No star rain'd light, but, pale and proud,
With blue-edged sickle Artemis cut her slow path thro' cloud.

8.

And when the weary dark was done,
Beyond my sphere of realm upsprang,
With smile that beam'd and harp that sang,
Strong Phoibos, piloting the Sun;
And conscious of him shining o'er,
I watch'd my black and watery floor
Wherein the wondrous upper-world is mirror'd evermore.

9.

When lo, there murmur'd on my brain,
Like sound of far-off waves a sound
That did my godlike sense confound
And kissed my eyelids down in pain;
And far above I heard the beat
Of musically falling feet,
Caught by the gnomes of earth and hurl'd down to my brazen seat.

10.

And I was 'ware that overhead
  Walk'd one whose very motion sent
  A sweet immortal wonderment
Thro' the deep dwellings of the Dead,
  And flush'd the seams of cavern and mine
  To gleams of gold and diamond shine,
And made the misty dews shoot up to kiss her feet divine.

11.

By Zeus, the beat of those soft feet
  Thrill'd to the very roots of Hell,
  Troubling the mournful streams that fell
Like snakes from out my brazen seat:
  Faint music reach'd me strange and slow,
  My conscious Throne gleam'd pale as snow,
A beauteous vision vaguely fill'd the dusky glass below.

12.

When I beheld in that dark glass
The phantom of a lonely maid,
Who gather'd flowers in a green glade
Knee-deep in dewy meadow-grass,
And on a riverside. Behold,
The sun that robed her round with gold,
Mirror'd beneath me wondrously, loom'd white and round and cold.

13.

Soft yellow hair that curl'd and clung
Throbbed to her feet in softest showers,
And as she went she gather'd flowers,
And as she gather'd flowers she sang:
It floated down my sulphurous eaves,
That faint sweet song of flowers and leaves,
Of vineyards, gushing purple wines, and yellow slanted sheaves.

14.

Darkling I mutter'd,." It were choice
Proudly to throne in solemn cheer
So fair a queen, and ever to hear
Such song from so divine a voice!"
And with the wish I upward breathed
A mist of fire that swiftly seethed
Thro' shuddering earth-seams overhead, and round her
warm knees wreathed.

15.

Whereon the caves of precious stones
Grew bright as moonlight thrown on death,
And red gold brighten'd, and the breath
Drew greenness moist from fleshless bones;
And every cave was murmuring:
"O River, cease to flow and sing,
And bear the tall bride on thy banks to the footstool
of thy king!"

16.

Then writhed the roots of forest trees
  In tortuous fear, till tremblingly
  Green leaves quaked round her. A sharp cry
Went upward from the Oreades;
  Low murmurs woke in bower and cave,
  With diapason in the wave:
The River eddied darkly round, obeying as a slave.

17.

Half stooping downward, while she held
  A flower in loosening fingers light;
  The quick pink fading from the white
Upon her cheek; with eyes that welled
  Dark pansy thoughts from veins that dart
  Like restless snakes round the honied heart,
And balmy breath that mildly blew her rose-leaf lips
  apart,—

18.

She listen'd—stately, yet dismay'd;
And dimly conscious of some change
That made the whispering place seem strange
And awful, far from human aid;
And as the moaning Stream grew near,
And whirl'd unto her with eddies clear,
She saw my shadow in his waves and shrank away in
fear.

19.

"Small River, flowing with summer sound,
Strong River, solemn Ades' slave,
Flow unto her with gentle wave,
And make an isle, and hem her round."
The River, sad with gentle worth,
Felt backward to that cave of earth
Where, troubled with my crimson eyes, he shudder'd
into birth.

20.

Him saw she trembling; but unseen,
Under long sedges lily-strew'd,
Round creeping roots of underwood,
Low down beneath the grasses green
Whereon she waited wondering-eyed,
My servant slid with stealthy tide:—
Then like a fountain bubbled up and foam'd on either side.

21.

And shrinking back she gazed in fear
On his wild hair, and lo, an isle—
Around whose brim waves rose the while
She cried, "O mother Ceres, hear!"
Then sprang she wildly to and fro,
Wilder than rain and white as snow.
"O honour'd River, grasp thy prize, and to the foot-stool flow!"

22.

One swift sun-beam with sickly flare
On white arms waving high did gleam,
What time she shriek'd, and the strong Stream
Leapt up and grasp'd her by the hair.
And all was dark. With wild heads bow'd
The forests murmur'd, and black cloud
Split speumy on the mountain tops with fire and portent loud!

23.

Then all was still as the Abyss,
Save for the dark and bubbling water,
And the far voice. "Bear Ceres' daughter
Unto the kingly feet of Dis!"
Wherefore I rose upon my throne,
And smote my kingdom's roof of stone;
Earth moan'd to her deep fiery roots—Hell answer'd with a groan.

24.

When swiftly waving sulphurous wings
The Darkness brooded down in fear
To listen. I, afar, could hear
The coming River's murmurings;
My god-like eyes with flash of flame
Peer'd up the chasm. As if in shame
Of his slave-deed, darkly and slow, my trembling servant came.

25.

The gentleness of summer light,
This Stream, my honour'd slave, possessed:
The blue flowers mirror'd in his breast,
And the meek lamps that sweeten night,
Had made his heart too mild to bear
With other than a gentle care,
And slow sad solemn pace, a load so violet-eyed and fair!

26.

Him saw I, as, thro' looming rocks,
He glimmer'd like a serpent gray
Whose moist coils hiss; then, far away,
Lo the dim gleam of golden locks,
Lo a far gleam of glinting gold,
Floating in many a throbbing fold,
What time cold ripples panted dark on queenly eyelids cold.

27.

Silently, with obeisance meet,
In gentle arms escorting well
The partner of eternal Hell,
Thus flow'd, not halting, to my feet
The gracious River with his load:
Her with dark arm-sweep he bestow'd
On my great footstool—then again, with sharp shriek, upward flowed.

28.

So fair, so fair, so strangely fair,
Dark with soft waters lay my love ;
And lo, I, Ades, stoop'd above,
And shuddering touch'd the yellow hair
That made my beaded eyeballs close—
Awful as sunshine. Cold as snows,
Pale-faced, dank-lidded, proud, she lay in wonderful repose.

29.

And all the lesser Thrones that rise
Around me, shook. With murmurous breath,
Their Kings shook off eternal death,
And with a million fiery eyes
Glared red above, below, around,
And saw me stooping fiery-crown'd ;
And the white faces of the damn'd arose without a sound.

30.

As if an awful sunbeam, rife
With living glory, pierced the gloom,
Bringing to spirits blind with doom
The summers of forgotten life,—
Those pallid faces, mad and stern,
Rose up in foam, and each in turn
Roll'd downward, as a white wave breaks, and seem'd to plead and yearn.

31.

What time this horror loom'd beyond,
Her soul was troubled into sighs:
Stooping, throned, crown'd, I touch'd her eyes
With dim and ceremonial wand;
And looking up, she saw and knew
An awful love which did subdue
Itself to her bright comeliness and gave her greeting due!

32.

"Welcome!"—The rocks and chasms and caves,
The million thrones and their black kings,
The very snakes and creeping things,
The very damn'd within the waves,
Groan'd "welcome;" and she heard—with light
Fingers that writhed in tresses bright,—
But when I touch'd her to the soul, she darkly rose
her height.

33.

While shadows of a reign eterne
Quench'd the fine glint in her yellow hair,
She rose erect more hugely fair,
And, dark'ning to a queenhood stern,
She gazed into mine eyes and thence
Drew black and subtle inference,
Subliming the black godhead there with sunnier,
sweeter sense.

34.

Low at her feet, huge Cerberus
Crouch'd groaning, but with glorious look
She strangely silenced him, and took
The throne sublime and perilous
That rose to hold her and upstream'd
Vaporous fire: the dark void scream'd,
The pale Eumenides made moan, with eyes and teeth that gleam'd.

35.

Behold, she sits beside me now,
A weighty sorrow in her mien,
Yet gracious to her woes—a queen;
The sunny locks about her brow
Shadow'd to godhead solemn, meet;
Throned, queen'd; but roundabout her feet,
Sweeten'd by gentle grass and flowers, the brackish waves grow sweet.

36.

And surely, when the mirror dun
  Beneath me mirrors yellowing leaves,
  And reapers binding golden sheaves,
And vineyards purple in the sun,
  When fulness fills the plenteous year
  Of the bright upper-world, I hear
The voice among the harvest-fields that mourns a
    daughter dear.

37.

"Lo, Ceres mourns the bride of Dis,"
  The old Earth moans, and rocks and hills,
  "Persephoné;" sad radiance fills
The dripping horn of Artemis,
  Silverly shaken in the sky;
  And a great frost-wind rushing by—
"Ceres will rob the eyes of Hell when seed-time
    draweth nigh."

38.

And in the seed-time after snow,
Down the long caves, in soft distress,
Dry corn-blades tangled in her dress,
The weary goddess wanders slow—
The million eyes of Hell are bent
On my strange queen in wonderment,—
The ghost of Iris gleams across my waters impotent!

39.

And the sweet Bow bends mild and bland
O'er rainy meadows near the light,
When fading far along the night
They wander upward hand-in-hand;
And like a phantom I remain,
Chain'd to a throne in lonely reign,
Till, sweet with greenness, moonlight-kiss'd, she wanders back again.

40.

But when afar thro' rifts of gold
  And caverns steep'd in fog complete,
  I hear the beat of her soft feet,
My kingdom totters as of old ;
  And, conscious of her sweeter worth,
  Her godhead of serener birth,
Hell, breathing fire thro' flowers and leaves, feels to
    the upper-earth.

II.

PAN.

It is not well, ye gods, it is not well!
Ay, hear me grumble—rouse, ye sleepers, rouse
Upon thick-carpeted Olympus' top—
Nor, faintly hearing, murmur in your sloth
"'Tis but the voice of Pan the malcontent!"
Shake the sleek sunshine from ambrosial locks,
Vouchsafe a sleepy glance at the far earth
That underneath ye wrinkles dim with cloud,
And smile, and sleep again!

Me, when at first
Light dawn'd on chaos like the ghost of form,
When the Deep murmur'd, and Eternity
Gave forth a hollow sound while from its voids
Ye blossom'd thick as flowers, and by the light

Beheld yourselves eternal and divine,—
Me, underneath the darkness visible
And calm as ocean when the cold Moon smoothes
The palpitating waves without a sound,—
Me, ye saw sleeping in a dream, white-hair'd,
Low-lidded, gentle, aged, and like the shade
Of the eternal self-unconsciousness
Out of whose law YE had awaken'd—gods
Fair-statured, self-apparent, marvellous,
Dove-eyed, and inconceivably divine.

Over the ledges of high mountains, thro'
The fulgent streams of dawn, soft-pillowëd
On downy clouds that swam in reddening streaks
Like milk wherein a crimson wine-drop melts,
And far beyond the dark of vague low lands,
Uprose Apollo, shaking from his locks
Ambrosial dews, and making as he rose
A muffled murmur as of numerous bees,
A whisper such as low winds weave in June.
Wherefore the darkness in whose depth I sat
Wonder'd: thro' newly-woven boughs the light,

Twinkling like dew-drops on a lion's mane,
Crept onward to mine eyelids unaware,
And fluttering o'er my wrinkled length of limb
Like a great butterfly above a snake,
Disturb'd me,—and I stirr'd, and open'd eyes,
Then lifted up my eyes to see the light,
And saw the light, and, seeing not myself,
Smiled!

Thereupon, ye gods, the woods and lawns
Grew populously glad with living things.
A rod of stone beneath my heel grew bright,
Writhing to life, and hissing drew swift coils
O'er the upspringing grass; above my head
A birch unbound her silver-shimmering hair,
Brightening to the gurgling notes of birds;
And far dim mountains hollow'd out themselves
To give forth streams, till down the mountain-sides
The loosen'd streams ran flowing. Then a voice
Came from the darkness as it roll'd away
Under Apollo's sunshine-sandall'd foot,
And the vague voice shriek'd "Pan!" and woods and
streams,

Sky-kissing mountains and the courteous vales,
Cried "Pan!" and earth's reverberating roots
Gave forth an answer, "Pan!" and stooping down
His fiery eyes to scorch me from my trance,
Unto the ravishment of his soft lyre
"Pan!" sang Apollo: when the wide world heard,
Brightening brightlier, till thro' murmurous leaves
Pale wood-nymphs peep'd around me whispering
"Pan!"
And sweeter faces floated in the stream
That gurgled to my ankle, whispering "Pan!"
And, clinging to the azure gown of air
That floated earthward dropping scented dews,
A hundred lesser spirits panted "Pan!"
And, far along an opening forest-glade,
Beating a green lawn with alternate feet,
"Pan!" cried the satyrs leaping. Then all sounds
Were hush'd for coming of a sweeter sound:
From the spilt chrism of the dawn I drank
Motion and thought and music unaware,
And rising up, with outstretch'd arms, I, Pan,
Look'd eastward, saw, and knew myself a god.

It was not well, ye gods, it was not well!
Star-guiders, cloud-compellers—ye who stretch
Ambrosia-dripping limbs, great-statured, bright,
Milky and fair-proportion'd, in a place
Thick-carpeted with grass as soft as sleep;
Who with mild glorious eyes of liquid depth
Subdue to perfect peace and calm eterne
The mists and vapours of the nether-world,
That curl up dimly from the nether-world
And make a roseate mist wherein ye lie
Soft-lidded, broad-foreheaded, stretch'd supine
In awful contemplations—ye great gods,
Who meditate your souls and find them fair—
Ye heirs of odorous rest—it was not well!—
For, with Apollo sheer above, I, Pan,
In whom a gracious godhead lived and moved,
Rose, glorious-hearted, and look'd down; and lo,
Goat-legs, goat-thighs, goat-feet, uncouth and rude,
And, higher, the breast and bowels of a beast,
Huge thews and twisted sinews swoll'n like cords,
And thick integument of bark-brown skin—
A hideous apparition masculine!

But in my veins a new and natural youth,
In my great veins a music as of boughs
When the cool aspen-fingers of the Rain
Feel for the eyelids of the earth in spring,
In every vein quick life; within my soul
The meekness of some sweet eternity
Forgot; and in mine eyes soft violet-thoughts
That widen'd in the eyeball unto the light,
And peep'd, and trembled chilly back to the soul
Like leaves of violets closing.

By my lawns,
My honey-flowing rivers, by my woods
Grape-growing, by my mountains down whose sides
The slow flocks thread like silver streams at eve,
By the grey comfort in the eyes of Zeus
When the soft murmur of my peaceful dales
Blows like a gust of perfume on his cheek,
There where he reigns, cloud-shrouded—by meek lives
That smoothe themselves like wings of doves and brood
Over immortal themes for love of me—
I swear it was not well.

Ay, ay, ye smile;—

Ye hear me, garrulous, and turn again
To contemplation of the slothful clouds
That curtain ye for sweetness. Hear me, gods!
Not the ineffable stars that interlace
The azure panoply of Zeus himself,
Have surer sweetness than my hyacinths
When they grow blue in gazing on blue heaven,
Than the white lilies of my rivers when
In leafy spring Selené's silver horn
Spills paleness, peace, and fragrance.—And for these,
For all the sensible or senseless things
Which swell the sounds and sights of earth and air,
I snatch some glory which of right belongs
To ye whom I revile: ay, and for these,
For all the sensible or senseless things
Which swell the sounds and sights of earth and air,
I will snatch fresher glory, fresher joy,
New joy and stranger glory, day by day,
Robbing your rights in heaven day by day,
Till from my dispensation ye remove
Darkness, and drought that parches thirsty skins,
The stinging alchemy of frost, the agues

That rack me in the season of black winds—
Till, bit by bit, my bestial nether-man
Peels off like bark, my green old age shoots up
Godhead apparent, and I know myself
Fair—as becomes a god!

Ay, I shall do!

Not I alone am something garrulous, gods!
But the broad-bosom'd Earth, whose countless young
Moan "Pan!" most piteously when ye frown
In tempests, or when thunder, waving wings,
Groans crouching from your lightning spears, and then
Springs at your lofty silence with a shriek!
Not I alone, huge horror masculine,
But earthquake-shaken hills, the courteous dales,
Blue rivers as they flow, and boughs of trees,
Yea, monsters, and the purblind race of men,
Grow garrulous of your higher glory, gods;
Yearning unto it moan my name aloud,
Climbing unto it shriek or whisper "Pan!"
Till from the far-off verdurous depths, from deep
Impenetrable woods whose wondrous roots
Blacken to coal or redden into sand,

I, stirring in this specious dream of mine,
Make answer—and they hear.
In Arcady
I, sick of mine own envy, hollow'd out
A valley, green and deep, then pouring forth
From the great hollow of my hand a stream
Sweeter than honey, bade it wander on
In blue and oily lapse to the far sea.
Upon its banks grew flowers as thick as grass,
Gum-dropping poplars and the purple vine,
Slim willows dusty like the thighs of bees,
And, further, milky stalks of corn and flax,
And, even further, on the smooth hill sides
White sheep and new-yean'd lambs, and in the midst
Mild-featured shepherds piping. Was not this
An image of your grander ease, O gods?
A faint sweet picture of your bliss, O gods?—
They thank'd me, those mild men, whose silken skins
Grew tough against the teeth of winds that crept
From dim frost-valleys far beyond the hills,
Keen winds that dying on my river's marge,
Only lent coolness to the lily, and made

The apple in the mouth bite chill and sour—
They thank'd me, those meek shepherds, with the smoke
Of crimson sacrifice of lambkins slain,
Rich spices, succulent herbs that savour meats;
And when they came upon me ere aware,
Walk'd sudden on my presence where I piped
By some lorn stream my mournful ditties old,
Cried "Pan!" and worshipp'd. Yet it was not well,
Ye gods, it was not well, that I, who gave
The harvest to these men, and with my breath
Thicken'd the wool upon the backs of sheep,
I, Pan, should in these purblind mortal forms
Witness a loveliness more gently fair,
Nearer to your dim loveliness, O gods!
Than my immortal wood-pervading self,—
Hideous to outward seeming, incomplete
As the vex'd earth who dips one balmy side
In sunshine, while the under side is dark
And ribb'd with ice unmelted,—quaintly shaped—
Carelessly blown on by the rosy Hours,
Who breathe quick breath and smile before they die—
Goat-footed, horn'd, a monster—yet a god.

By wanton Aphroditê's velvet limbs,
By Herê's haughty jealous eyes, by him
Who glorified the lover in the god,
And came to Danäe's bower in golden rain—
I swear, ye amorous gods, it was not well!—
Down the long vale of Arcady I chasèd
A wood-nymph unapparell'd and white-limb'd,
From gleaming shoulder unto foot a curve
Delicious, like the bow of Artemis:
A gleam of milky moonlight on her limbs;
Within her veins a motion as of waves
Moon-led and silver-crested to the moon;
And in her heart a sweetness such as fills
Uplooking maidens when the virgin orb
Witches warm bosoms into snows, and gives
The colourable chastity of flowers
To the tumultuous senses curl'd within.
Her, after summer noon, what time her foot
Startled with moonlight motion milky stalks
Of hyacinths in a dim forest glade,—
Her saw I, and, uplifting eager arms,
I rush'd around her as a rush of boughs,

My touch thrill'd thro' her, she beheld my face,
And like a gnat it stung her, and she fled.

By Hermes' pandar-wand, it was not well!—
Down the green glade, along the verdurous shade,
She screaming fled and I pursued behind:
By Zeus, it was as though the forest moved
Behind her, following; and with shooting boughs,
And bristling arms and stems, and murmurous leaves,
It eddied after her—my underwood
Of bramble and the yellow-blossom'd furze
Flung its thick growth around her waist, my trees
Dropt thorns before her, and my growing grass
Put forth its green and sappy oils and slid
Under her feet; until, with streaming hair
Like a well'd sunshine torn 'mid scars and cliffs,
Pale, breathless, and long-throated like a swan,
With tongue that panted 'tween the foamy lips
As the red arrow in a tulip's cup,
She, coming swiftly on the river-side,
Into the circle of a sedgy pool
Plunged knee-deep, shrieking. Then I, thrusting arms

To grasp her, touch'd her with hot hands that clung
Like burrs to the soft skin; while, writhing down
Even as a fountain lessens gurglingly,
She cried to Artemis, "Artemis, Artemis,
Sweet goddess, Artemis, aid me, Artemis!"
And o'er the laurels on the river-side,
Dark and low-fluttering, Daphne's hidden soul
Breathed fear like hoar-frost, echoing "Artemis";
When lo, above the sandy sunset rose
The silver sickle of the green-gown'd witch,
Which flickered thrice into a pallid orb,
And thrice flash'd white across the forest leaves,
And—lo, the change ye wot of: melting limbs
Black'ning to oozy sap of reeds, white hands
Waving aloft and putting forth green shoots,
The faint breath-bubbles circling in a pool,
Last, the sharp voice's murmur dying away
In the low lapping of the rippling pool,
The melancholy motion of the pool,
And the faint undertone of whispering reeds.

By Latmos and its shepherd, was it well?

By smooth-chin'd Syrinx, was it well, O gods?
Yet mark. What time the pallid sickle wax'd
Blue-edged and luminous o'er the black'ning west,
I, looming hideous in the smooth pool, stooped
And pluck'd seven wondrous pipes of brittle reeds
Wherein the wood-nymph's soul still fluttered faint;
And these seven pipes I shaped to one, wherein
I, Pan, with ancient and dejected head
Nodding above its image in the pool,
And large limbs stretch'd their length on shadowy banks,
Did breathe such weird and awful ravishment,
Such symmetry of sadness and sweet sound,
Such murmurs of deep boughs and hollow cells,
That neither bright Apollo's hair-strung lute,
Nor Heré's queenly tongue when her red lips
Flutter to intercession of love-thoughts
Throned in the counsel-keeping eyes of Zeus,
Nor airs from heaven, blow sweetlier. Hear me, gods!
Behind her veil of azure, Artemis
Turn'd pale and listen'd; mountains, woods, and streams,

And every mute and living thing therein,
Marvell'd, and hush'd themselves to hear the end—
Yea, far away, the fringe of the green sea
Caught the faint sound and with a deeper moan
Rounded the pebbles on the shadowy shore.
Whence, in the season of the pensive eve,
The earth plumes down her weary, weary wings;
The Hours, each frozen in his mazy dance,
Look scared upon the stars and seem to stand
Stone-still, like chisell'd angels mocking Time;
And woods and streams and mountains, beasts and
birds,
And serious hearts of purblind men, are hush'd;—
While music sweeter far than any dream
Floats from the far-off silence, where I sit
Wondrously woven about with mighty boughs—
Through which the moon peeps faintly, on whose leaves
The unseen stars sprinkle a diamond dew—
And shadow'd in some water that not flows,
But, pausing, spreads dark waves as smooth as oil
To listen!

Am I over-garrulous, gods?

Thou pale-faced witch, green-kirtled,—thou whose
light
Troubles the beardless shepherd where he sleeps
On Latmos,—am I over-garrulous?
Nay, then, pale huntress of my groves, I swear
The lily and the primrose 'neath thy heel
Savour as fair as thee, as pure as thee,
Drinking the pallid glamour of thy speed;
And on the cheeks of marriageable maids
Dwells a faint pallor enviably sweet,
Sweet as thy sweetest self, yet robb'd from thee.
Snow-bosom'd lady, art thou proud?—Then hark . .
When last in the cool quiet of the night
Thou glimmeredst dimly down with thy white nymphs,
And brush'd these dewy lawns with buskin'd foot,
I, Pan the scorn'd, into an oak-tree crept,
And holding between thumb and finger—thus—
A tiny acorn, dropt it cunningly
In the small nest beneath thy snow-heap'd breasts,
And you—you paused in tumult, cried aloud,
Then redden'd like a rose from breast to brow,
Sharp-crimson like a rose from breast to brow,

And trembled, aspen-hearted, timorous
As new-yean'd lambs, and with a young doe's cry
Startled amazed from thine own tremulous shade
Faint-mirror'd in the dark and dewy lawn!

Ha, turn your mild grand eyes, O gods, and hear!
Why do I murmur darkly, do ye ask?
What do I seek for, yearn for?—Why, not much.
I would be milky-limb'd and straight and tall
And pleasant-featured, like Apollo there!
I would be lithe and fair as Hermes is;
And, with that glittering sheath of god-like form,
Trust me, I'd find for it a wit as keen
As that which long ago did prick and pain
The thin skin of the Sun-god. I would be
Grand and fine-statured as becomes a god,
A godlike sight conceived harmoniously,
A stately incarnation of my sweet
Pipings in lonely places. There's the worm!

Ay, ay, the mood is on me—I am aged,
White-bearded, and my very lifted hands

Shake garrulously—and ye hear, and smile.
By the faint undertone of this blind Earth,
Swooning towards the pathway of the Sun
With flowery pulses, leafy veins, whene'er
She hears in intercession of new births
My voice miraculous melancholy old,—
I swear not I alone, a sensible god,
Shall keep these misproportions, worse than beast's;
While woods and streams, and all that dwell therein,
And merest flowers, and the starr'd coils of snakes,
Yea, purblind mortal men, inhale from heaven
Such dews as give them heavenly seemliness,
Communicably lovely as the shapes
That doze on high Olympus.

Is it well?

Ye who compel the very clouds to forms
Beauteous and mildly beauteous, ere my rain
Rends their white vestments into flowers to make
My peaceful vales look lovely,—gods, great gods,
I ask ye, is it well?—Ye answer not.
But Earth has answer'd, and all things that grow,
All things that live, all things that feel or see

The interchanges of the sun and moon;
And with a yearning palpable and dumb,
Yet conscious of some glory yet unborn,
Of some new wonder yet to come, I, Pan,
Prophesy.
In the time to come,—in years
Across whose vast I wearily impel
These antient, blear'd, and humble-lidded eyes,—
Some law more strong than I, yet part of me,
Some power more piteous, yet a part of me,
Shall hurl ye from Olympus to the depths,
And bruise ye back to that great darkness whence
Ye blossom'd thick as flowers; while, I—I, Pan—
The ancient haunting shadow of dim earths,
Shall slough this form of beast, this wrinkled length,
This hard integument of dark-brown skin,
Yea, cast it from my foot as one who shakes
A worthless garment off; and lo, beneath,
Mild-featured manhood, manhood eminent,
Subdued into the glory of a god,
Sheer harmony of body and of soul,
Wondrous, and inconceivably divine.

Wherefore, ye gods, with this my prophecy
I sadden those sweet sounds I pipe unseen.
From dimly lonely places float the sounds
To haunt the nervous regions of the air,
Whatever changeful season ye vouchsafe
To all broad worlds which, hearing, whisper "Pan!"
And thence they reach the hearts of lonely men,
Who wearily bear the burthen and are pain'd
To utterance of fond prophetic song,
Who singing smile, because the song is sweet,
Who die, because they cannot sing the end.

It is my care to keep the graves of such
Thick-strewn and deep with grass and precious flowers
Such as ye slumber on; and to those graves,
In sable vestments, ever comes the ghost
Of my forgot and dumb eternity,
Mnemosyne; but what she broods on there
I know not, nor can any wholly know,
Mortal or god. The seasons come and go,
In their due season perish rocks and trees,
In their due season are the streams drain'd dry;

Earth dumbly changes, and those lonely men,
Less blind than purblind mortals, sing and die;
But still, with hooded and dejected head,
Above those graves ponders Mnemosyne;
While I remain to pipe my ditties old,
And my new prophecy, in ancient woods
And by the margins of unfortunate pools,—
My wondrous music dying afar away
Upon the fringes of the setting sun.

III.

THE NAIAD.

1.

DIAN white-arm'd has given me this cool shrine,
Deep in the bosom of a wood of pine:
    The silver-sparkling showers
    That hive me in, the flowers
That prink my fountain's brim, are hers and mine;
  And when the days are mild and fair,
    And grass is springing, buds are blowing,
    Sweet it is, 'mid waters flowing,
  Here to sit, and know no care,
    'Mid the waters flowing, flowing, flowing,
  Combing my yellow, yellow hair.

2.

The ounce and panther down the mountain-side
Creep thro' green darkness in the eventide;
And at the fountain's brink
Casting great shades they drink,
Gazing upon me, tame and sapphire-eyed;
For, awed by my pale face, whose light
Gleameth thro' sedge and lilies yellow,
They, lapping at my fountain mellow,
Harm not the lamb that in affright
Throws in the pool so mellow, mellow, mellow,
Its shadow small and dusky-white.

3.

Oft do the fauns and satyrs, flusht with play,
Come to my coolness in the hot noon-day.
Nay, once indeed, I vow
By Dian's truthful brow,
The great god Pan himself did pass this way,
And, all in festal oak-leaves clad,
His limbs among these lilies throwing,
Watch'd the silver waters flowing,

Listen'd to their music glad,
  Saw and heard them flowing, flowing, flowing,
And ah! his face was worn and sad!

4.

Mild joys around like silvery waters fall;
But it is sweetest, sweetest far of all,
    In the calm summer night,
    When the tree-tops look white,
To be exhaled in dew at Dian's call,
  Among my sister-clouds to move
    Over the darkness earth-bedimming,
    Milky-robed thro' heaven swimming,
  Floating round the stars above,
    Swimming proudly, swimming, proudly swimming,
  And waiting on the Moon I love.

5.

So tenderly I keep this cool green shrine,
Deep in the bosom of a wood of pine;
    Faithful thro' shade and sun,
    That service due and done

May haply earn for me a place divine
Among the white-robed deities
That thread thro' starry paths, attending
My sweet Lady, calmly wending
Thro' the silence of the skies,
Changing in hues of beauty never ending,
Drinking the light of Dian's eyes.

IV.

THE SATYR.

1.

THE trunk of this tree,
  Dusky-leaved, shaggy-rooted,
  Is a pillow well suited
To a hybrid like me,
  Goat-bearded, goat-footed;
For the boughs of the glade
  Meet above me, and throw
A cool pleasant shade
  On the greenness below;
And yet, all the while,
  Thro' the boughs I can see
A star, with a smile,
  Looking at me.

2.

The frolic and fun
Of the day are done;
Not a sound
  Breaks the wood's repose,
  Save the leaves that close,
Dusky and brown'd,
With a whisper around,
And hiving me neatly
  In this calm place,
Where 'tis dark completely,
  Leave one small space
  Above—where the face
Of my star shines sweetly.

3.

Full length I lie,
  On this mossy tree-knot,
With face to the sky,
  The vast blue I see not;
And I start in surprise
  From my dim half-dream,

With the moist white gleam
Of the star in mine eyes:
So strange does it seem
That the star should beam
From her milky throne
On this forest nook
Of all others, and look
Upon me alone:
Ay, that yonder divine
Soft face
Should shine
On this one place;
And, when things so fair
Fill the earth and air,
Should choose to be,
Night after night,
The especial light
Of a monster like me!

4.

Why, all day long,
I run about

Mid a madcap throng,
  And laugh and shout;
I laugh and sing,
  I tumble and roll,
Like a thing
  Without a soul.—
Silenus grips
  My ears, and strides
On my shaggy hips,
    And up and down
    In an ivy crown
  Drunkenly rides;
And when in a doze
His eyelids close,
  Off he tumbles, and I
Can his wine-skin steal,
I drink—and feel
  The grass roll—sea-high!
Then my courage swells
  Into juicy fruit,
And with shouts and yells,
Down mossy dells

Which reel underfoot,
I stagger after
The wood-nymphs fleet,
Who with mocking laughter
And smiles retreat
Upon glimmering feet;
And just as I clasp
A yielding waist,
With a cry embraced,
——Gush! it melts from my grasp
Into water cool,
And—bubble! trouble!
Seeing double!
I stumble and gasp
In some icy pool!

5.

All suborn me,
Flout me, scorn me!
Drunken joys
And cares are mine,
Romp and noise,

And the dregs of wine;
And whene'er in the night
Diana glides by
The spot where I lie,
With her maids green-dight,
I must turn my back
In a rude affright,
And blindly fly
From her shining track;
Or if only I hear
Her bright footstep draw near,
Fall with face to the grass,
Not breathing for fear
Till I feel her pass.

6.

I am—
I know not what:
Neither what I am,
Nor what I am not—
I seem to have rollick'd,
And frolick'd,

In this wood for ay,
With a beast's delight
Romping all day,
Dreaming all night!
Yet I seem
To remember awaking
Just here, and aching
With the last forsaking
Tender gleam
Of a droll strange dream.—
When I lay at mine ease,
With a sense at my heart
Of being a part
Of the grass and trees
And the scented earth,
And of drinking the bright
Subdued sunlight
With a leafy mirth:
Then behold, I could see
A wood-nymph peeping
Out of her tree,
And closer creeping,

Timorously
Looking at me!
And still, so still,
I lay until
  She trembled close to me,
  Soft as a rose to me,
And I leapt with a thrill
  And a shout, and threw
Arms around her, and press'd her,
Kiss'd her, caress'd her,—
  Ere she scream'd, and flew.

7.

Then I was 'ware
  Of a power I had—
To drink the air,
    Laugh and shout,
    Run about,
  And be consciously glad—
So I follow'd the maiden
  Neath shady eaves,
Thro' groves deep-laden

With fruit and leaves,
Till, drawing near
To a brooklet clear,
I shuddering fled
From the monstrous shape
There mirrorëd—
Which seem'd to espy me,
And grin and gape,
And leap up high
In the air with a cry,
And fly me!

8.

Whence I seem to have slowly
Grown conscious of being
A thing wild, unholy,
And foul to the seeing.—
But ere I knew aught
Of others like me,
I would lie, fancy-fraught,
In the greenness of thought,
Beneath a green tree;

And seem to be deep
  In the scented earth-shade
  'Neath the grass of the glade,
In a strange half-sleep :
When the wind seem'd to move me,
  The cool rain to kiss,
The sunlight to love me,
  The stars in their bliss
To tingle above me ;
And I crept thro' deep bowers
That were sparkling with showers
  And sprouting for pleasure,
And I quicken'd the flowers
  To a joy without measure—
Till my sense seem'd consuming
  With warmth, and, upspringing,
I saw the flowers blooming,
  And heard the birds singing!

9.

Yet I seem,
In spite of the dream,

To have dwelt for ay
  In a mad delight,
Romping all day,
  Dozing all night—
My rude face roughen'd
  By rain and breeze,
My dark skin toughen'd
  Like the barks of trees,
My wild heart gushing
  With dew-like fun,
My beast's brain flushing
  Like fruit in the sun!

10.

Wherever I range,
  Thro' the greenery,
That vision strange,
  Whatsoever it be,
  Is a part of me
Which suffers not change—
    A part
  Of my blood and heart.—

The changes of earth,
Water, air, ever-stirring,
Disturb me, conferring
My sadness or mirth:
Wheresoever I run,
I drink strength from the sun;
The wind stirs my veins
With the leaves of the wood,
The dews and the rains
Mingle into my blood.
I stop short
In my sport,
Panting, and cower,
While the blue skies darken
With a sunny shower;
And I lie and hearken,
In a balmy pain,
To the tinkling clatter,
Pitter, patter,
Of the rain
On the leaves close to me,
And sweet thrills pass

Thro' and thro' me,
  Till I tingle like grass.
When lightning with noise
  Tears the wood's green ceiling,
When the black sky's voice
  Is terribly pealing,
I hide me, hide me, hide me,
  With wild averted face,
  In some terror-stricken place,
While flowers and trees beside me,
  And every streamlet near,
Darken, whirl, and wonder,
Above, around, and under,
And murmur back the thunder
  In a palpitating fear!

II.

Ay; and when the earth turns
  A soft bosom of balm
To the darkness that yearns
  Above it, and grows
  To dark, dewy, and calm

Repose,—
I, apart from rude riot,
Partake of the quiet
The night is bequeathing,
Lie, unseen and unheard,
In the greenness just stirr'd
By its own soft breathing—
And my heart then thrills
With a soft sensation
Like the purl of rills
Down moonlit hills
That loom afar,
With a sweet sensation
Like the palpitation
Of yonder star!

12.

Ho, to climb
To that sublime
White light above me,
Who, of all the big sky
Chose that one place on high,

And seems to love me!
For all the night
My face I turn to her,
And softly yearn to her,
And meekly bright,
With faint flame stirring,
She thrills for delight
Of the bliss she's conferring.

13.

Thro' yonder bough
Her white ray twinkles;
And on my brow
She silently sprinkles
A dewy rain,
That lulls my brain
To a dream of being
Under the ground,
Blind to seeing,
Deaf to sound,
Drinking a dew
That drops from afar,

And feeling unto
  The sweet pulse of a star,
Who is beckoniug me
Though I cannot see!
And of suddenly blooming
  Up into the air,
And, swooning, assuming
  The shape I wear!
While all fair things
  Fly night and day from me,
Wave bright wings,
  And glimmer away from me!

14.

  If I must climb
  To that light sublime,
And never reach her,—
  But increase in self-fearing,
  Self-seeing, self-hearing,—
I beseech her
To resolve me anew
Into the dew

Of this wood-nest green—
This dew,
Which (for aught I knew!)
I may have been—
Then, while I lie low,
Unconscious and dumb,
Exhale me slowly
To her bosom holy—
Whence (for aught I know!)
I may have come.

15.

—She shines above me,
And heareth not,
Though she smiles on this spot
And seems to love me.
Here I lie aloof,
Goat-footed, knock-kneed,
A monster, indeed,
From horns to hoof;
And the star burns clearly
With pearl-white gleam—

Have I merely
  Dream'd a dream?
Am I nought,
In form or thought,
  Save the monster I seem?
Have I dwelt for ever
  In the wood with the rest,
Changing never,—
  A monster, at best?

16.

'Tis a puzzle, to ponder
    If yonder
Soft light, changing not,
  Will always be shining
  Thro' the intertwining
Boughs on this one spot?
The seasons change,
  Leaves redden and fall—
Some influence strange
  Is at work, over all:
Can a thing such as I

Remain while the fair
Shapes of earth, water, air,
Come and die?
And will the time come
When the star there will see
No fellow stretch'd dumb
On the trunk of this tree,
While his thoughts come and flee
Drowsily?
And will she take flight,
When no more she can be
The bright
Especial delight
Of a monster like me?

17.

—Did she hear me, I wonder?—
She trembles upon
Her throne—and is gone!
The boughs darken under,
Then thrill, and are stirr'd
By the notes of a bird.

The green grass brightens
  With pearly dew,
And the whole wood whitens
  As the dawn creeps thro'.—
"Hoho!"—that shout
Flung the echoes about
  The boughs, like balls!
    Who calls?—
'Tis the noisy rout
Of my fellows upspringing
  From sleep and dreaming,
To the birds' shrill singing,
  The day's soft beaming:
While the whole wood moves
  As the Sun-god dawns,
  They are beating the lawns
With their noisy hooves;
And they madly go
To and fro,
  Though o' nights they are dumb.
Hoho! hoho!
  I come! I come!

Hark !—to the cry
They reply :
"Ha, there, ha !"
"Hurrah !"—"hurrah !"
  And starting afraid
At the cries,
  In the depths of the glade
Echo replies—
"Ho, there !"—"ho, there !"—
By the stream below there
  The answer dies.

V.

VENUS CYTHEREA.

—•—

1.

Tell me, thou many-finger'd Frost,
Coming and going like a ghost
    In leafless woods forsaken—
O Frost, that o'er him lying low
Drawest the garment of the snow
    From silver cloud-wings shaken,
And round bare boughs with strange device
Twinest fantastic leaves of ice—
    When will Adon waken?
Lo, dawn by dawn I rise afar
Beside Apollo in his car,
    And, far below us wreathing,

Thy fogs and mists are duskly curl'd
Round the white silence of the world,
    Like to its own deep breathing;
But crimson thro' the mist our light
Foameth and freezeth, till by night
    Snow-bosom'd hills we fade on—
The pallid god, at my desire,
Gives unto thee a breath of fire
    To reach the lips of Adon.

2.

Tell me, thou bare and wintry World,
Wherein the wingëd flowers are curl'd
    Like fairies darkly dozing—
O World, within whose lap he lies,
With thy quick earth upon his eyes,
    In dim unseen reposing,
Husht underneath the wind and storm,
Still rosy-lipt in darkness warm—
    Are Adon's eyes unclosing?
Lo, dawn by dawn I rise afar
Beside Apollo in his car,

Keen-pricking as we go by
Sharp tiny rifts in ice and snow
Where ice-drops roll and melting show
Shapes for flowers to grow by.
Wonderful creatures of the light
Flutter above thee, hanging bright
Faint pictures glen and glade on;
The pallid god, at my desire,
Hideth in cloudy snows his fire,
To reach the sleep of Adon.

3.

Tell me, thou spirit of the Sun,
Radiant-lock'd and glorious one,
Strong, constant, unforsaking—
Sun, by whose shadier side I sit,
And search thy face, and question it,
Conferring light and taking—
Thou whose eternal brightness throws
The shadow-hours on his repose,—
Is my Adon waking?
Lo, dawn by dawn I rise afar

Beside thee in thy flaming car,
    Thou ever-constant comer!
And flashing on the clouds that break
Around our path thy sunbeams make
    A phantom of the summer.
O breathe upon the Moon, that she
May use her magic witchery
    When snowy hills we fade on,
That, in the dark, when thou art gone,
She speed the resurrection,
    And stir the sleep of Adon!

4.

Tell me, O silver-wingëd Moon,
That glidest to melodious tune
    Ice-sparkling pallid skies up,—
O Moon, that to the sunset grey,
Drinking faint light that fades away,
    Liftest immortal eyes up,
And walking on, art thro' the night
Troubled to pain by that strange light,—
    When will Adon rise up?

Lo, dawn by dawn I rise afar
Beside Apollo in his car,
    Imploring sign or token ;
But night by night such pale peace beams
Upon his slumber, that it seems
    Too beauteous to be broken !

O gentle goddess, be not cold—
But, some dim dawn, may we behold
    New glory hill and glade on,
The leaves and flowers alive to bliss,
And, somewhat pale with your last kiss,
    The smiling face of Adon !

VI.

SELENE THE MOON.

1.

I HIDE myself in the cloud that flies
  From the west and drops on the hill's grey shoulder,
And I gleam thro' the cloud with my panther-eyes,
  While the stars turn paler, the dews grow colder;
I veil my naked glory in mist,
  Quivering downward and dewily glistening,
Till his sleep is as pale as my lips unkist,
  And I tremble above him, panting and listening.
As white as a star and as cold as a stone,
  Dim as my light in a sleeping lake,
With his head on his arm he lieth alone.
    And I sigh "Awake!
Wake, Endymion, wake and see!"

And he stirs in his sleep for the love of me;
 But on his eyelids my breath I shake:
  "Endymion, Endymion!
  Awaken, awaken!"
 And the yellow grass stirs with the mystic moan,
  And the tall pines groan,
 And Echo sighs in her grot forsaken
  The name of Endymion!

2.

A foamy dew from the Ocean old,
 Whence I rise with shadows behind me flying,
Drops from my sandals and glittereth cold
 On the long spear-grass where my love is lying;
My face is dim with departed suns,
 And my eyes are dark from the depths of ocean,
A starry shudder throughout me runs,
 And my pale cloud stirs with a radiant motion,
When the darkness wherein he slumbers alone
 Ebbs back from my brightness, as black waves break
From my shining ankle with shuddering tone;
  And I sigh "Awake!

Wake, Endymion, wake and hear!"
And he stirs in his sleep with a dreamy fear,
And his thin lips part for my sweet sake:
"Endymion, Endymion!
Awaken, awaken!"
And the skies are moved, and a shadow is blown
From the Thunderer's throne,
And the spell of a voice from Olympus shaken
Echoes "Endymion!"

3.

Then under his lids like a balmy rain
I put pale dreams of my heavenly glory;—
And he sees me lead with a silver chain
The tamed Sea-Tempest white-tooth'd and hoary;
And he sees me fading thro' forests dark
Where the leopard and lion avoid me in wonder,
Or ploughing the sky in a pearly bark,
While the earth is dumb with my beauty under!
Then he brightens and yearns where he lies alone,
And his heart grows dumb with a yearning ache,
And the thin lips part with a wondering moan,

As I sigh "Awake!
Wake, Endymion, wake and see
All things grow bright for the love of me,
With a love that grows gentle for thy sweet sake!
Endymion, Endymion!
Awaken, awaken!"
And my glory grows paler, the deep woods groan,
And the waves intone,
Ay, all things whereon my glory is shaken
Murmur "Endymion!"

4.

Aï! The black earth brightens, the Sea creeps near
When I swim from the sunset's shadowy portal;
But he will not see, and he will not hear,
Though to hear and see were to be immortal:
Pale as a star and cold as a stone,
Dim as my ghost in a sleeping lake,
In an icy vision he lieth alone,
And I sigh "Awake!
Wake, Endymion, wake and be
Divine, divine, for the love of me!"

And my odorous breath on his lids I shake :
 "Endymion, Endymion!
 Awaken, awaken!"
But Destiny sits on his cloud-shrouded throne,
 And heareth my moan,
And his stern lips form not the hope-forsaken
 Name of Endymion.

VII.

IRIS THE RAINBOW.

1.

'Mid the cloud-enshrouded haze
  Of Olympus I arise,
With the full and rainy gaze
  Of Apollo in mine eyes;
But I shade my dazzled glance
  With my dripping pinions white
Where the sunlight sparkles dance
  In a many-tinctured light:
My foot upon the woof
  Of a fleecy cloudlet small,
I glimmer thro' the roof
  Of the paven banquet-hall,

And a soft pink radiance dips
  Thro' the floating mists divine,
Touching eyes and cheeks and lips
  Of the mild-eyed gods supine,
And the pinky odour rolls
  Round their foreheads, while I stain,
With a blush like wine, the bowls
  Of foam-crusted porcelain:
Till the whole calm place has caught
  A deep gleam of milky fire—
When I darken to the thought
  In the eyes of Zeus the Sire.

2.

Then Zeus, arising, stoops
  O'er the ledges of the skies,
Looking downward, thro' the loops
  Of the starry tapestries,
On the evident dark plain
  Speck'd with wood and hill and stream,
On the wrinkled tawny main
  Where the ships, like snowflakes, gleam;

And with finger without swerve,
  Swiftly lifted, swiftly whirl'd,
He draws a magic curve
  O'er the cirrus of the world;
When with waving wings display'd,
  On the Sun-god's threshold bright
I upleap, and seem to fade
  In a humid flash of light;
But I plunge thro' vapours dim
  To the dark low-lying land,
And I tremble, float, and swim,
  On the strange curve of the Hand:
From my wings, that drip, drip, drip,
  With cool rains, shoot jets of fire,
As across green capes I slip
  With the thought of Zeus the Sire.

3.

Thence, with drooping wings bedew'd,
  Folded close about my form,
I alight with feet unview'd
  On the ledges of the storm;

For a moment, cloud-enroll'd,
  Mid the murm'rous rain I stand,
And with meteor eyes behold
  Vapoury ocean, misty land;
Till the thought of Zeus outsprings
  From my ripe mouth with a sigh,
And unto my lips it clings
  Like a shining butterfly;
When I brighten, gleam, and glow
  And my glittering wings unfurl,
And the melting colours flow
  To my foot of dusky pearl;
And the ocean mile on mile
  Gleams thro' capes and straits and bays,
And the vales and mountains smile,
  And the leaves are wet with rays,—
While I wave the humid Bow
  Of my wings with flash of fire,
And the Tempest, crouch'd below,
  Knows the thought of Zeus the Sire.

VIII.

ORPHEUS THE MUSICIAN.

I sat of old beside a stream new-born
  Out of the loamy loins of mountains cold
And it was garrulous with dreams forlorn
  And mystic legends old.

Wherefore the secrets of the peaks and caves
  With the faint music in mine ears were blended;
And as the stream slid down to ocean-waves,
  I heard and comprehended.

Into a moss-soft silence dim and deep
  I sank with murmurous sighs and drowsy nods:
Then, opening eyes, like one who starts from sleep,
  I sang the birth of gods.—

A gleaming shoulder cut the stream, and lo!
  The Naiad rose to hear me melodise;
She, like a blue-vein'd lily white as snow,
  Floated, with half-closed eyes.

And, ere my eyes were 'ware, the boughs around
  Were populous with faces strange and glad,
That droopt pale under-lips and drank the sound,
  And grew divinely sad.

Far down the glade where many shadows slept,
  Stain'd purple with the swollen leaves of vine,
I saw Silenus:—liquid music crept
  Into his blood, like wine:

Tiptoe, like one who fears to break a spell,
  He crept to me, with eyeballs blank as glass—
Not drawing breath till, at my knees, he fell
  Full length upon the grass:

Then, leaning his fork'd chin upon his hand,
  He listen'd, dead to drunken joy and strife,
And lo! his face grew smooth and soft and bland
  With some sublimer life.

Goat-footed fauns and satyrs one by one,
With limbs upon the sward at random thrown,
Gather'd, and darken'd round me in the sun
Like moveless shapes of stone.

And straight before me, o'er the green hillside,
Quaint shapes across the sunset linger'd bright,
Till the white eyes of heaven opening wide
Swam dewy, in delight.

The dusky twilight rustled o'er the place,
Full of sweet airs and odour and cool shade,
But music made a lamp of every face
In the swart forest-glade.

Then, in a pearly shower of cool moonbeams,
Upsprang Silené to her azure arc,
Scattering light and silence and sweet dreams
On weary eyelids dark :

The music sadden'd, the moist greenwood stirr'd
And sigh'd, the moonlight clothed us in its veil,
And stooping down the milky goddess heard
The music and grew pale.

For as they listen'd, satyrs, nymphs, and fauns
  Grew credulous of their immortality—
Yea, the weird spirits of the woods and lawns,
  Gross, weak, and vile to see—

Whence her pure light disturb'd them, and they strove
  With wild scared looks to fright away the charm;
But the bright light grew brighter, from above
  Shaken with pearly arm.

They could not fly, they could not move nor speak,
  The music held them like a hand of strength—
They hid their faces, wild, abash'd, and weak,
  And, list'ning, writhed full length.

The Naiad lifted up her dewy chin,
  And heard, and knew, and saw the light with love,
Made peaceful by a purity akin
  To that faint face above.

And countless beauteous spirits of the shade
  Were conscious of themselves and felt no fear;
Far Echo, nestling in green silence, made
  Answer that all could hear.

Till, when I ceased to sing, the satyrs rush'd
  Back to their sports, to riot and carouse;
Self-fearful faces of the forest blush'd
  And rustled into boughs;

Lastly, Silenus to his knees upcrept,
  Rubb'd his blear'd eyelids puffy like the vine,
Stared blankly round him, vow'd that he had slept,
  And bawl'd aloud for wine.

IX.

POLYPHEME'S PASSION.

Ho, Silenus!—no one here!
  The kitchen empty, the flocks in stalls,
  The red fire flickering over the walls,
And—a young kid spitted—dainty cheer!
Ho, Silenus!—tipsy old reveller,
Soft-zone-unloosener, bright-hair-disheveller,
Where are you hiding, you tipsy old hound you,
With your beard of a goat and your eyes of a lamb?

SILENUS.

Ho, Cyclops!

POLYPHEME.

He mocks me! Where are you, confound you?

SILENUS.

Patience, sweet master, here I am!—

POLYPHEME.

Rise! or with my great fist I'll put an end to you;
The dregs of my great flagon have been warming you—
You're drunk, sow-ears. I find there's no reforming you,
Tho' six round moons I've tried to be a friend to you.
Once more divinely warming those old veins,
  Chirping like grasshoppers at every pore,
Foaming as warm as milk among your brains,
  Gushing like sunshine in your dry heart's core,
Runs the pink nectar of my vines. It stains,
  Flowing from that bald head, this grassy floor—
Too sweet for earth to drink, unmeet for thee,
Fit only to be quaffed by gods like me!

SILENUS.

Cyclops!

POLYPHEME.

Jump up, then, quickly. Nay, no more.
Follow me to this rocky eminence,

Cool-cushion'd with the yellow moss, from whence
  We can at ease behold
The cloud-stain'd greenness of the ocean sleek,
Rounding its smooth mild waves into the creek,
  Speckled with sparkling jewels manifold,
And, far away, one melting patch of gold.
  Now, sit!—Nay, nearer, higher—here, above
My shoulder. Turn your face on mine, Silenus!
Fear not:—being fill'd with the sweet milk of Venus,
  You're a fit counsellor for one in love;
And, as I'm in a talking humour, why—
Suppose we chat a little at our leisure.

SILENUS.

With pleasure!
The subject?

POLYPHEME.

One alone beneath the sky,
Old man, is worthy of the conversation
And serious consideration
  Of such a god as I!
Now, guess the name of that sweet thing?

SILENUS.

With ease.
Bacchus, the god to whom these aged knees
Bend gloriously impotent so often,
And in whose luscious pool
I dip hot mouth and eyes, and soak and soften
The yoke of your strong rule.

POLYPHEME.

A thing a thousand times more beautiful!

SILENUS.

I know no thing more beautiful than he
When, dripping odours cool,
Deep-purpled, like a honey-bosom'd flower
For which the red mouth buzzes like a bee,
He bursts from thy deep caverns gushingly,
And throws his pleasure round him in a shower,
And sparkles, sparkles, like the eyes that see,
In sunshine, murmuring for very glee
And bursting foamy bubbles until sour
Lips tremble into moist anticipation
Of his rich exultation!

POLYPHEME.

Has little Bacchus, whom you praise so, power
  To unnerve these mighty limbs, make this one Eye
Rain impotent tears, hurl this gigantic bulk
Down on its stubborn knees—nay, make me skulk
  And fume and fret, and simper oaths, and sigh,
Like tiny mortal milking-maids who sulk
  In dairies, frothing yellow like their cream?
Could Bacchus, once let loose to fight and fly,
  Do all these things to sinewy Polypheme?

SILENUS.

Assuredly!

POLYPHEME.

By this right hand, you lie!—
I am a god, great-statured, strong, and born
  Out of Poseidon's nervy loins divine;
I laugh the wrath of Zeus himself to scorn;
And when I rise erect on Aetna's horn
  My shadow on the faint sea-hyaline
Falls like a cloud wherein the winds drop still
And white-wing'd ships move slowly without will.

Shall bulk so wondrous and so grand as mine
Yield to the miserable god of wine!

SILENUS.

Certainly not.

POLYPHEME.

Never!—by Pallas' spear,
At whose sharp touch the plump god leaps and flies,
While startled Revel shrieks with haggard eyes!
Never, by Hermes, whom the drunken fear,
But whose quick fingers pilfer not the wise!

SILENUS.

Whom shall we praise, O Cyclops?

POLYPHEME.

You shall hear—
Tell me, did you ever see a,—
Ever hear a, ever hear a,—
Either far away or near, a—
Nymph so sweet as Galatea?

SILENUS.

Never!

POLYPHEME.

'Tis false, old man! she is not fair;—
Those weeds that under ocean rot at ease
Into dark dreams o' the flowery earth, and there
Put purples in the sea-nymph's sunny hair
Are fairer: she is changeable as these.
She is as wanton as the perfumed fays
That dimple on the windless sea and dally,
Musically,
With the puff'd sails of ships becalm'd for days.

SILENUS.

True, Cyclops, she is fickle; and by her
Whose amorous breath blew the Greek host to Troy,
I have seen fairer!

POLYPHEME.

Dotard! Driveller!
Not her the false Idalian shepherd-boy,
With silken string, like a tame heifer, led—
Nay, not lush Aphroditè, whose blue eyne,
Pink-lidded, smiled on their unhallow'd bed—

Is half so fair, so precious, so divine,
As Galatea!

SILENUS.

Exactly what I said.

POLYPHEME.

Her voice hath gentle sweetness, borrowëd
From soft tide-lispings on the pebbly sand,
'Tis like the brooding doves in junipers;
White as a shell of ocean is her hand,
Wherein, like ocean sound, the pink blood stirs!
Her hair excels the fruitage of the beech
Wherein the sun runs liquid gleam on gleam;
Her breasts are like two foamy bowls of cream,
A red straw-berry in the midst of each;
And the soft gold-down on her silken chin
Is like the under-side of a ripe peach—
A dimple dipping honeyly therein!

SILENUS.

Her eyes—

POLYPHEME.

Profane them not!—For their sweet fire is

Wondrous and various as the Bow
Drawn over rainy ledges dripping low
By many-colour'd Iris—
From whose bright end, plunged the dark waters
 under,
Woven with the tapestries of her sea cave,
And dying hue by hue on the green wave,
They may have drunk a portion of their wonder.
But oh, what tongue can tell
Their glory inexpressible?
You seem to see the music of the ocean
Folded within them, as within a shell,
And gently stirring with a violet motion,
Until it drops unto the lips, and there
Flutters in perfumed accents on the air!
Nor this alone. They change as the sea changes,
In hues as various as the ringdove's dyes:
Whatsoever sweet and strange is
Flashes across them with a quick surprise.
Now, like a bright
Bird startling thro'
The rainy greenness of a shadowy glade,

And scattering the pearly drops of dew
With quick sharp fluttering light
That dying deepens the shade,
A fancy leaps up glad beyond control—
Then fades along their depths into the soul.
Now, in their troubled orbs rise multiform
Wild pictures of sky-tempest and sea-storm;
And her wild eyes droop brightly on her breast
Till it is troubled like a thing distrest,
As lightnings seem to wake the waves white-crested.
There's nothing, nothing, nothing anywhere,
Humanely or divinely manifested,
That can with them compare;
And yet they seem to share
The glory of all things, palpably invested
With all the wonders of earth, ocean, air.
But in their softest mood
You watch the pale soul tremulously brood
On those bright orbs whose fire the dark sea cools,
And there it trembles, as the moonlight flows
On seas just stirr'd by their own deep repose
And throbbing, throbbing, into silver pools!

SILENUS.

O eloquent Cyclops, pause, and breathe a space !—
Few eyes save thine, few eyes of earth, have plainly
Seen this immortal Galatea's face ;
For she you worship is of that fair race
Whom mortal vision dreams of, but seeks vainly—
For they comb and they comb
Their yellow locks,
Under the foam,
Among weedy rocks !
And they sing unseen
In their sea-caves green,
And gaze at the white sun overhead
Whose pale ray saddens their dripping curls,
Or the moon that glimm'ring in ocean's bed
Leaves her motion for ever in pools of pearls !

POLYPHEME.

Chirrup not, wine-sponge !—Am not I a god ?
Cannot this eye peer to Olympus' helm ?
Does not the great sea, trembling at my nod,
Hush itself humbly around this my realm ?

SILENUS.

It does, O Cyclops!

POLYPHEME.

Save, of course, when I
Hurl rocks and trees down on the shuddering ships,
And, while I loom above the waves, my lips
Roar terrible defiance at the sky.

SILENUS.

Precisely.

POLYPHEME.

Ask not, then, the when and how;
But turn your ancient gaze
On the broad wonder of my noble brow,
Thence drop it, in a natural amaze,
Down the steep mountain to my sinewy feet,
Round which the lambs, as small as snowflakes, bleat;
Now, tell me—am I fair?

SILENUS.

Most fair!

POLYPHEME.

Your fears
Lie to my strength a hollow lie, Silenus!

SILENUS.

By all the love that there exists between us,
By doves that perch on Bacchus' vine-wreath'd ears,
I swear thou art most beautiful!

POLYPHEME.

Again:
Have those blurr'd eyeballs noticed that of late
My air has grown more solemn, more sedate,
More bountiful to those I hold in chain
To watch my flocks, and more compassionate;
As if I struggled underneath the weight
Of some indefinite pain?
That I have learn'd to tremble and to blush,
To droop this eyelid modestly, to flush
All over at the tiniest whispering sound,
To pick small dainty steps upon the ground
As if I saw and seeing fear'd to crush

Some crawling insect or the crimson-crown'd
Small daisy-flower that, whensoe'er I pass,
Shuts up its little leaves upon the grass
And thinks the shadowy eve has stolen down!

SILENUS.

Cyclops!—These things I saw, but fear'd to question;
Nay, with a blush I own it—do not frown!—
I set your trouble down as indigestion.
For neither unmilk'd kids, nor lambs stall-fed,
Nor sucking-swine with pippins in their teeth,
Nor ox-thighs with green herbs engarlanded,
Nor foamy curds wherein hot apples seethe,
Nay, not the parsley-flavour'd tongues of sheep,
Could tempt o' late thy dainty appetite;
But lying on the mountain out of sight
Of melancholy you have drunken deep;
While down among the yellow pastures moaning
With lambs new-yeaned, where thy cool streamlets run,
We saw you loom above us, mighty one!
Like a great cloud dark-sleeping in the sun,—

And heard you, like the monstrous seas intoning,
Melodiously groaning!

POLYPHEME.

Ay me! ay me!

SILENUS.

Be calm, sweet Polypheme!
The eagle poised o'er yonder cropping lamb
Flew scared, at that big cry.

POLYPHEME.

Ay me! I am
Lost, swallow'd up, absorbed into a dream!
Thro' the swift current of my frame gigantic
Eddies a frantic
Consuming fire. I am not what I seem.
For Galatea I refuse all food,
For Galatea I grow weak and wild
And petulant-featured as a sickly child;
For Galatea I, in desperate mood,
Seek out green places in this solitude,
And close my eyes, and think I am a curl

Tingling, tingling, lightly
Against the snow-heap'd bosom swelling whitely!

SILENUS.

One should not break his heart for any girl.

POLYPHEME.

Ay me! I close my eyes in a sweet woe,
And dream that I am little, fair, and sweet,
For a small goddess's embraces meet,
Nor huge, nor rough. It was not always so!
Of old, Silenus, this great awful Me
Was swoll'n with glory at the contemplation
Of its enormity in yonder sea;
I revell'd in the roar and consternation,
When, grasping rocks with frantic acclamation,
Round this frowning, Ætna-crowning head I whirl'd them,
Tremendously, stupendously, and hurl'd them
On the passing fleets below;
And from under came the thunder of vessels crushed asunder,

And the shriek, faint and weak, of the mortals in their
wonder,
And the sea rolled underneath, and the winds began to
blow,
And above the desolation, drunk with rage, I took my
station,
With my waving arms expanded and my crimson eye
aglow,
And to earth's reverberation,
Roar'd "Ho! ho! ho!"

SILENUS.

Cyclops! sweet Cyclops!—you appal me!

POLYPHEME.

Fear not!
I am as weak as the eagle's callow young;
Yet listen, mild old man, and interfere not.
One summer-day, when earth and heaven rung
With thunders, and the hissing lightning stung
With forkëd meteor tongue
The green smooth living ocean till it shriek'd—
I stood aloft on Ætna's horn and wreak'd

My cruel humour with a monstrous glee:
When lo! from out the rainy void did flit
Bright Iris, and with tremulous foot alit
On this my mountain, touching even me
With her faint glory: for a moment, she
Paused shudd'ring high above me: then with fleet
Footstep slid downward till she reach'd my feet;
And there, with many-tinctured wings serene,
She waved the seas to silence, and, beguiled
By her mild message, the dark ocean smiled—
A palpitating lapse of oily green,
With silvery glimmers here and there between
The shadows of the clouds that, dewy and mild,
Parted and flutter'd:—when, with radiant head
Plunging among the bulbous mists, she fled.
But, as the vapours fleam'd away, behold!
I saw far down upon the brown sea-strand
A nymph who held aloft in pearly hand
A white-tooth'd comb, and comb'd her locks of gold
Over a dank and shipwreck'd sailor-lad,—
On whose damp eyelids a faint radiance lay,
Robb'd from some little homestead far away,

Some silent hearth that wearily would wait,
For that faint smile which left it desolate,
And hush itself and watch and yearn and pray.
Oh! tenderly she comb'd her locks of gold,
Over that gently-sleeping sailor-lad,
Stretch'd 'mid the purple dulse and rockweed cold;
And all the while she sang a ditty sad,
To deep division of the wave that roll'd
Up to her feet, like a huge snake that springs,
At two bright butterflies with golden wings:

Marinere, O Marinere,
  Waken, waken!
  Sleep-o'ertaken,
Look upon me, with no fear,
Look, and see, and hear:
Underneath the white-tooth'd waves,
Sleep your comrades in their caves;
Coral grottoes are their bed,
Purple plants stir overhead.
All around black weeds are twined,
Frozen still without a wind;

And the sea-nymphs in distress
Pluck dark flowers all odourless,
Growing deep in caverns clear,
Gently to bestrew their bier.
Under the sea
They sleep—ah me!
They have slept for many a year.

Marinere, O Marinere,
  Wake not, wake not,
  Slumber break not,
Close your eyelids with no fear,
Do not see, nor hear!
Far above the silence deep,
Where your gentle comrades sleep,
Rolls the sea and foams the storm,
Horrors thicken, demons swarm,
And the sea-nymphs, lightning-led,
Flash about white-garmented;
But below the Storm-god's frown,
Sleep the shipwreck'd fathoms down—
Waves they hear not on the bier,

Foam-bells hang in every ear!
Under the sea
They sleep—ah me!
They shall sleep for many a year.

SILENUS.

That was the song she sang?

POLYPHEME.

It was. But ill
Those tender accents fill
This rocky breast, whose distant roar
Frightens those white waves seaward from the shore.
For they trembled, tinkling, twining,
For melodious combining,
While her yellow locks fell shining
To her knees,
While the Storm with bright eyes glistening,
Thro' its cloud-veil looking at her,
Delay'd breathlessly and listening
On the ledges of the seas:
And in the sun she sat her,

While her voice went pitter-patter,
Pitter-patter, like the clatter
Of bright rain on boughs of trees!
Then ho! with my great stride,
Down the steep mountain side,
I sprang unto her, with mine arms extended!
Her bright locks gleam'd afraid,
Like a sunbeam trapt in shade,
In my deep shadow, and the music ended:
And she rose erect to fly,
Panting, moaning, and her cry
Met the lifted cry of Ocean, and they blended!
While earth reel'd under,
Downward I bore,
With step of thunder,
On to the shore;
And in shrieking amaze,
With eyes fasten'd in fear—
Like a star's firm gaze
When a cloud draws near—
On the horror that came
With an eye of flame,

She leapt to the water,
  All woebegone;
  And her bright locks shone
And tript and distraught her,
But the water caught her
  And push'd her on!
From billow to billow,
  With wild locks streaming
    And tangling oft;
From billow to billow,
  Dark-green, or gleaming
    Like doves' wings soft,
From billow to billow,
Panting and screaming,
With white hands beaming
    And waving aloft!
Then, coming hideous
    On to the tide,
I spurn'd the perfidious
    Foam aside,
And follow'd her, dashing
    Thro' storm sublime,

Flashing, crashing,
Splashing splashing
    On the seaweed's slippery slime!
The billows clomb up,
With flash of foam up,
    My loins and thighs;
Till they gleam'd and fleam'd,
With clangor and anger,
And around me upstream'd
    With their wild white eyes!
Till panting, choking,
Dripping and soaking,
With nostrils smoking,
I halted, spitting,
    Spurting, chin-deep,
And saw her sitting
Where gulls were flitting
    Far out on the deep;
And all around her with gentle motion
One smooth soft part of the murmurous ocean
    Had gone to sleep!
Then waving her hands,

And shaking her locks,
To the ocean sands,
To the purple rocks
Under the foam,
To the sea-caves brown,
She sank to her home,
Down! down! down! down!
And the sea grew black
In her shining track,
And the waters green
Darken'd afar;
And the one thing seen
Was the steadfast star
Of my round Eye red,
Rolling immense
With a pain intense
In my rocky head,
Mid the white foam wreathing
Around wind-led,
And the great sea seething
Down to deep breathing,
Like a monster panting, on its sandy bed!

SILENUS.

Most musical Cyclops!

POLYPHEME.

Hush!—Unto the beach
I wearily strode, with great head bow'd, and dragg'd
Foot-echoes after me; and with no speech,
On yonder shore, weedy and wet and cragg'd,
I stood, and in an agony of pain
Look'd out with widening eyeball on the main.
Lo! far away a white wind glided dim
O'er the cloud-cover'd bright'ning ocean-rim,
And violet shadows here and there were trail'd
Over the waters: then behold the sun
Flasht pale across the waste, and one by one,
Like sea-gulls dripping rain, rose ships white-sail'd.
All else was silence, save monotonous moan
Of the broad-chested billows, till the warm
Light kindled all things, and I loomed alone—
The one huge cloud remaining of the storm;
And in the awfulness of that strange hour
A change came over my big throbbing breast,

And the soft picture of the calm had power
To move my mountainous bulk with vague unrest!—

SILENUS.

Weep not, O Cyclops—lest thy tears should roll
Down oceanward and brain the grazing sheep!

POLYPHEME.

Ay me, ay me, the passion in my soul!
Ay me, her glory haunts me, and I weep!—
Gentle Silenus!

SILENUS.

Beautiful Cyclops!

POLYPHEME.

Nay,
Not beautiful, Silenus?

SILENUS.

But *I* say
Most beautiful, and fearlessly I dare
Utter the truth. By him whose shoulders bear

The great round world, by Atlas' self, I swear
Thou art most fair!

POLYPHEME.

O, I would give away the world to be
As soft, as sweet, as fleecy-limb'd as she,
As tiny and as tender and as white
As her mild loveliness!
With two soft eyes such as mere men possess,
Two pretty little dewy eyes, that might
Interpret me aright!

SILENUS.

Amazement!—Polypheme, whom vast Poseidon
Spawn'd upon Thoosa in the salted brine,
Thou who canst strangle fleets, and sit astride on
Ætna and roar your origin divine!
Wrong not thyself, thy beauty, and thy sire!
See! where your mighty shadow stretches wide
Down the steep mountain side,
And see! that eyeball of immortal fire!
Had wanton Helen, Paris' love-sick toy,

Beheld thee, Polypheme,
Hill-haunting Echo had not found a theme
In ruin and the ten years' war of Troy.

POLYPHEME.

And is it so?

SILENUS.

By Ganeymede bright-eyed,
By—by—

POLYPHEME.

Enough—let us return. I stood,
When she had flown, in meditative mood;
Then, raising up my resinous hands, I cried:
"O thou from whose huge loins I darkling came,
King of all ocean and its wondrous races,
Return, return, the nymph to my embraces,
Or, thro' thy lips ooze-dripping, name her name!"
And o'er the sands did a low murmur creep,
Whispering, 'Galatea;' and, deep-pain'd,
I vaguely knew, like one who dreams in sleep,
She was a goddess of the sacred deep,
Not to be lightly won or roughly gain'd.

SILENUS.

O pitiful! and you—

POLYPHEME.

In the dim birth
Of the strange love that stirs my hid blood's fountains,
As unborn earthquakes trouble springs in mountains,
I look'd abroad upon the fair green earth;
And lo, all things that lived, all things that stirr'd,
Unto the very daisy closing up
In my great shade its crimson-tippëd cup,
And the small lambs, and every little bird,
Seem'd to abhor and dread, avoid and fear me;
And in an agony of hate for all,
I cried "How can a thing so sweet, so small,
So gentle, love me—or be happy near me?"
Whereon I sadly clomb the cliffs and made
A looking-glass of yonder ocean, where
Startled by my long shade
The silver-bellied fishes rose afraid;
But with a lover's hand I smooth'd my hair
To sleekness, parting it with care,

And husht the rugged sorrow of my brow—
Then, stooping softly o'er the dimpled mirror,
I shaped my face to a sweet smile—as now!

SILENUS.

O agony! help, help, ye gods! O terror!
Hide me!

POLYPHEME.

What ails thee? Ha!

SILENUS.

O Ocean's child—
Cyclops! My heart, with admiration rent,
Fainted and cried with its deep ravishment
Because you look'd so beauteous when you smiled!

POLYPHEME.

Thou liest!—and (ay me) you shrunk in fear
As silly younglings shrink at something hateful;
Yet tremble not:—to a lorn lover's ear,
E'en flattery so base as thine is grateful.
Ay me, ay me—I am

A great sad mountain in whose depths doth roam
My small soul, wandering like a gentle lamb
That bleats from place to place and has no home;
But prison'd among rocks
Can just behold afar
A land where honey-flowing rivers are
And gentle shepherds with their gentle flocks:
For even so my timid soul looks round
On beauteous living things—that creep and seem,
To this vast Eye, like insects on the ground—
From whose companionship 'tis shut and bound
Within this mountain of a Polypheme!

SILENUS.

Most melancholy Cyclops, be consoled!

POLYPHEME.

My heart is like those blubbery crimson blots
That float on the dank tide in oozy spots;
It is as mild as patient flocks in fold.
I am as lonely as the snowy peak
Of Dardonos, and, like an eagle, Love

Stoops o'er me, helpless, from its eyrie above,
And grasps that lamb, my Soul, within its beak.
Nay, on the margin of the waters where
She comes and goes like a swift gull, I sit
Above these flocks, and rake my little wit
To pipe upon the misty mountain air
Ditties as tender as a shepherd man,
Perch'd on a little hillock, half asleep,
Surrounded by his silly stainless sheep,
Pipes with mild pleasure and no definite plan
In fields Arcadian. [*He sings.*

White is the little hand of Galatea,
  That combs her yellow locks with dainty care;
Bright is the fluttering hand of Galatea,
  When tangled, like a dove, in sunny hair.
Meet is Galatea—sweet is Galatea—
  Ay, so sweet!
Complete is Galatea, from her feathery fingers fair
  To her small white mice of feet!
The billows huge and hoar cease to rumble and to
  roar,

When the white hands wave above them, like doves
that shine and soar,
And, as gentle, from the shore, I adore, and implore
Galatea!

Ho, that these limbs were meet for Galatea
With soft pink kisses sweetly to enfold!
Ho, had I two small eyes, that Galatea
Might there my gentle gentle heart behold!
Clear is Galatea—dear is Galatea—
Ay, so dear!
No peer has Galatea, but her bosom is so cold
And her eyes so full of fear!
When the great sea wildly rise, there is terror in her
eyes,
And she trembles in sweet wonder, like a bird that
storms surprise,—
And before my tender cries, and my sighs, swiftly flies
Galatea!

Under the white sea-storm sits Galatea
While overhead the sea-birds scream in flocks,

In deep-gréen darkness sitteth Galatea,
Combing out sunshine from her golden locks!
Rare sits Galatea—fair sits Galatea—
Ay, so fair!
Ho, there sits Galatea, in the shade of purple rocks
Mid the fountain of her hair!
Ho, would I were the waves, on whose crest the tempest raves,
So might I still the tempest that my raging bulk outbraves,
For the dark-green stillness laves, and enslaves, and encaves
Galatea!

SILENUS.

Comfort, O Cyclops, comfort! There is sure
Some remedy for such a wound as this:
Red wine, I say again: the plump God's kiss
Is sweeter far than honey, rich and pure.

POLYPHEME.

Alas, not he whose temples Artemis
Bound with weird herbs and poison-snakes that hiss

But sting not—wise Asclepios—could cure!
For evermore, Silenus, when my brain
Lies in a dream just conscious of its pain,
And my full heart throbs tenderly and rockingly,
Far out upon the bosom of the main
She flashes up, green-kirtled, and laughs mockingly.
Thrice has her smile enticed me to the chin
Thro' the great waves that round me bite and bark,
And gleam'd away and left me in the dark.
Alas, that I must woo and never win!
Alas, that I am foul while she is fair!
Alas, that this red Eye, my only one,
Like a brown lizard looking on the sun,
Turns green in her bright mist of yellow hair!

SILENUS.

Majestic Cyclops! Heir of the huge Sea!
God-like,—like those great heavens that oversheen us!
One-eyed, like the bright Day! Wilt thou by me,
Thy servant, be advised?

POLYPHEME.

Speak on, Silenus.

SILENUS.

Behold!—Beneath the many-tinctured west hid,
Fades Phœbus crimson-crested,
And the faint image of his parting light
On the deep Sea broad-breasted
Fades glassily; while down the mountain height
Behind us, slides the purple shadow'd Night.
Come in!—and from your cellar iced by springs
Drag forth the god of wine,
And listen to him as he chirps and sings
His songs delicious, dulcet, and divine:
Throned in the brain, magnificently wise,
And blowing warmly out thro' kindled eyes
All vapours vapid, vain, and vague.
Seek the god's counsel, Cyclops, I beseech you;
'Tis he alone, if once his magic reach you,
Can cure Love's panting heat or shivering ague.

POLYPHEME.

He cannot make me fair!

SILENUS.

Phoo!—He will teach you

To lift your dreamy gaze from the soft sod,
And rise erect, big-hearted, self-reliant,
On Ætna's horn, with leathern lungs defiant—
No minnow-hearted grampus of a god!
And—then in the quick flush and exultation
Of that proud inspiration,
Wine in his nostrils, Polypheme will be
In Polypheme's own estimation
A match for any girl on land or sea.
Then, furiously, gloriously rash,
Grasp Opportunity, that, passing by
On the sheet-lightning with a moment's flash,
Haunts us for ever with its meteor eye;
And—grasp the thing you pant for now in vain,
Ay, hold her fast, and if you choose intreat her—
But, if she still be deaf to your sad pain,
Why, hearken to the mad god in your brain,
And make a meal of trouble—that is, eat her!

X.

PENELOPE.

Whither, Ulysses, whither dost thou roam,
Roll'd round with wind-led waves that render dark
The smoothly-spinning circle of the sea?
Where dost thou linger? Whither dost thou drag
The silken chain thou fastenedst round my neck
When to the porch of thy inclement realm,
With blushing face turn'd backward, first I came,
Trembling and treading fearfully on flowers?
Lo, Troy has fallen, fallen like a tower,
And the mild sun of a less glorious day
Gleams faintly on its ruins. One by one,
Swift as the sparkle of a star the ships
Have dipt up gladly from the under-world,
And plumëd warriors, standing in their prows,

Stretching out arms to wives and little ones
That crowd with seaward faces on the beach,
Have flung their armour off and leapt and swam
Ere yet the homeward keels had grazed the sand.
And these—the gaunt survivors of thy peers—
Have landed, shone upon by those they love,
And faded into happy happy homes;
While I, the lonely woman, hugging close
The comfort of thy individual fame,
Still wait and yearn and wish towards the sea;
And all the air is hollow of my joy:
The seasons come and go, the hour-glass runs,
The day and night come punctual as of old;
But thy deep strength is in the solemn dawn,
And thy proud step is in the plumëd noon,
And thy grave voice is in the whispering eve;
And all the while, amid this dream of thee,
In restless resolution oceanward,
I sit and ply my sedentary task,
And fear that I am lonelier than I know.

Dear Lord, the rose you took away with you

From this nice cheek, flusht proudly on thy face
When far away around thee glittering
The Trojan phalanx brighten'd; ay, but still
The lily-flower you left my cheek instead,
To be a token pure betwixt us twain,
Grows like the sampler coarse-complexionëd.
For in the shadow of thy coming home
I sit and weave a weary housewife's web,
Pale as a silkworm in the cone; all day
I sit and weave this weary housewife's web,
And in the night with fingers swift as frost
Unweave the weary labour of the day.
Behold now, I am mock'd!—Suspicion
Mumbles my name between his toothless gums;
And whilo I ply my sedentary task,
They come to me, mere men of hollow clay,
Rat-eyed, and viper-lip'd, they come to me,
And whisper odious comfort, and upbraid
The love that follows thee where'er thou art,
That follows, and perchance, with thy moist cheek,
Dips on the watery bottom of the world.
They come, Ulysses, and they seek to rob

Thy glory of its weaker wearier half.
They tell me thou art dead ; nay, they have brought
To these cold ears that bend above the web
Whispers that thou, no wiser than thy peers,
Hast pluckt upon the windy plain of Troy
A flower thou shrinest in a distant land,
A chamber'd delicacy drowsy-eyed,
Pink-lidded, wanton, like the queen who witch'd
The fatal apple out of Paris' palm.

And I—and I—ah me, I rise my height,
In matron majesty that melts in tears,
And chide them from me with a tongue that long
Has lost the trick of chiding : what avails ?
They heed me not, rude men, they heed me not ;
And he thou leftest here to guard me well,
He, the old man, is helpless, and his eyes
Are yellow with the dim gold-minting lie
That thou art dead. O husband, what avails ?
They gather on me, till the sense grows cold
And huddles in upon the steadfast heart ;
And they have dragg'd a promise from my lips

To choose a murderer of my love for thee,
To choose at will from out the rest one man
To slay me with his kisses in the dark,
Whene'er the weary web at which I work
Be woven: so, all day, I weave the web;
And in the night with fingers like a thief's
Unweave the silken sorrow of the day.

The years wear on. Telemachus, thy son,
Who, when in the old time we paused athirst
With utterness of wedded joy, upsprang
Between us like a fountain, grows and grows,
Upgurgling like a fountain jet by jet,
And murmuring somewhat sadly, but withal
Sparkling when shone upon. He is thy son:
More woman-like than thee, less strong of limb,
Yet worthy thee; and likest thy grave mood,
When, in old time, among these fields, thine eye
Would kindle on a battle far away,
And thy proud nostrils, drinking the mild breath
Of tannëd haycocks and of slanted sheaves,
Swell suddenly, as if a trumpet spake.

Much sojourn with my weeping widowhood
Has taught the boy a young man's gentleness;
Courteous beyond his years unto my grief
He helps me daily, till by night sweet dream
Hangs on his eyelids like a violet,
A violet with its shadow on his cheek.
Hast thou forgotten how of old he loved
To toy with thy great beard, and sport with thee,
And how, in thy strong grasp, he leapt and seem'd
A lambkin dandled in a lion's paw?
About his cradle men who sought the stars
Sprinkled mild prophecies like dewy flowers,
Flowers sweet with light and wet with woman's tears;
And, now his long limbs lengthen white as milk,
Those stars seem true, for never have I seen
So kind a growth in sweeter smelling soil.
Behold now, how his burning boy-face turns
With impotent words beyond all blows of arm
On those rude men that rack thy weary wife!
Then turns to put his comfort on my cheek,
While sorrow brightens round him—as the grey
Of heaven melts to silver round a star!

Return, Ulysses, ere too late, too late :
Return, tall wedded warrior, return :
Return, return, and end the weary web !
For day by day I look upon the sea
And watch each ship that dippeth like a gull
Across the long straight line afar away
Where heaven and ocean meet ; and when the winds
Swoop to the waves and lift them by the hair,
And the long storm-roar gathers, on my knees
I pray for thee. Lo, even now, the deep
Is garrulous of thy vessel tempest-tost ;
And on the treeless upland grey-eyed March,
With blue and humid mantle backward blown,
Plucks the first primrose in a blustering wind.
The keels are wheel'd unto the ocean sand
And eyes look outward for the homeward bound.
And not a marinere, or man or boy,
Scum'd and salt-blooded from the boisterous sea,
Touches these shores, but straight I summon him,
And bribe with meat and drink to tell good news,
And question him of thee. But what avails ?
Thou wanderest ; and with leaden arms I search

The blank circumference of my pale loss.

My very heart has grown a timid mouse,
Peeping out, fearful, when the house is still.
Breathless I listen thro' the breathless dark,
And hear the cock counting the leaden hours,
And, in the pauses of his cry, the deep
Swings on the flat sand with a hollow clang;
And, pale and burning-eyed, I fall asleep
When, with wild hair, across the wrinkled wave
Stares the sick Dawn that brings thee not to me.

Ulysses, come! Ere traitors leave the mark
Of spread wine-dripping fingers on the smooth
And decent shoulders that now stoop for thee.
I am not young nor happy as of old,
When, awed by thy male strength, my face grew dark
At thy grave footfall, with a serious joy.
Much hope has dwelt within my heart so long
Its settled habit seems despair; but O!
Let amiable ocean smile around,
Green-sparkling on thy dripping homeward oars,

And thou come stately to mine arms, my soul
Shall drink such utter loveliness and joy,
Such loveliness and joy in that first flash
Of faces gloriously agonized
With doubtful recognition,—that the kiss
Wherewith I hunger round thee eager-arm'd,
Than a young bride's first kiss shall sweeter be,
And have more power to make thee young again
Than Helen's, when she stang the hip of Greece.
I am not young and beauteous as of old;
And much I fear that when we meet thy face
May startle darkly at the work of years,
And turn to hide a disappointed pang,
And then, with thy grave pride, subdue itself
Into such pity as is love stone-dead.
But thou, thou too, art old, dear lord—thy hair
Is threaded with the silver foam—thy heart
Is weary from the blows of cruel years;
And thou wilt need a tender woman's hand
To smooth the salt blood to a settled peace;
And more, the gathering strength of this thy son
To make thee young once more,—that you in him

May fight your noble battles o'er again,
And love again when he has learnt to love,
And follow him upward with a father's eye,
Until the mists close round him and he halts
Upon the cope of manhood, stooping down
To sow good deeds, and sweetness, on thy grave.

Return, return, Ulysses, ere I die!
Upon this desolate, desolate strand I wait,
Wearily stooping o'er the weary web—
An alabaster woman, whose fix'd eyes
Stare seaward, whether it be storm or calm.
And ever, evermore, as in a dream,
I see thee gazing hither from thy ship
In sunset regions where the still seas rot,
And stretching out great arms whose shadows fall
Gigantic on the glassy purple sea;
And ever, evermore, you come to me,
And evermore your coming far away
Aches on the burning heartstrings tentative,
And evermore you come not,—and I age.

XI.

SAPPHO:

ON THE LEUCADIAN ROCK.

1.

O SWEET, sweet, sweet!
While the Moon, with her dove's eyes fair,
And her beautiful yellow-hair,
And the green Snake coil'd around her silvery feet,
Walk'd dumbly up above in the jewell'd air
Waving her luminous wings,
To sit upon this crag above the sea
Clasp'd close, so close, to thee,
Pale with much yearning, while the murmurings
Of the great waters seem'd to waft to me
The name of Phaon,
To whisper Phaon, Phaon,

Phaon, Phaon, Phaon, with deep intoning,
    Hushfully, hushfully moaning!

2.

    O bliss, bliss, bliss!
Though the Moon look'd pale in the sky,
On thy passionate heart to lie,
    To cling to thy burning lips with kiss on kiss,
Faintly watching the butterfly stars swim by
    In the track of that queenly Moon;
And in a dream, clasp'd close, so close, to thee,
To list and seem to be
    A portion of the faint monotonous tune
Made for its mistress by the white-tooth'd sea,
    That whisper'd Phaon,
    Phaon, Phaon, Phaon,
Phaon, Phaon, Phaon, while Dian darkening
    Stoop'd hushfully, hushfully, harkening!

3.

    O pain, pain, pain!
While the Moon, in a sky as clear

As of old, walks on, and I hear
    Her palpitating foot on the shudd'ring main,
While, under my feet, the green sea-snake creeps near
    Hissing with scales that gleam,
To stand upon this crag beside the sea,
And dream, and dream, of thee—
    With clench'd white hands, set teeth, and robes that stream
Behind me in the wind, while audibly
    The waves moan Phaon,
    Shriek Phaon, Phaon, Phaon,
Phaon, Phaon, Phaon, with deep intoning,
    Tumultuously, tumultuously groaning!

4.

    O rest, rest, rest!—
While the Moon with her virgin light
Thro' eternities of night
    Dumbly paces on to the east from the west,—
To mingle with the waves that under the height
    Murmur along the shore,
To mix my virgin love, my agony,

Into the restless sea
    That Dian strives to comfort evermore,
To cling to those white skirts and moan of thee,
    O Phaon, Phaon,
    Restless for love of Phaon,
Phaon, Phaon, Phaon, with ceaseless motion,
    Yet soothed by the soother of Ocean!

XII.

A VOICE FROM ACADEME.

OVER this azure poplar glade
The sunshine, fainting high above,
Ebbs back from woolly clouds that move
Like browsing lambs and cast no shade;
And straight before me, faintly seen
Thro' emerald boughs that intervene,
The visible sun turns white and weaves
Long webs of silver thro' the leaves.
The grassy sward beneath my foot
Is soft as lips of lambs and beeves.
How cool those lilies at the root
Of yonder tree, that dimly dance
Thro' dews of their own radiance!

Yonder I see the river run,
Half in the shade, half in the sun ;
And as I near its rushy brink
The sparkling minnows, where they lie
With silver bellies to the sky,
Flash from me in a shower and sink.
I stand in shadows cool and sweet,
But in the mirror at my feet
The heated azure heavens wink.

All round about this shaded spot,
Whither the sunshine cometh not,
Where all is beautiful repose—
I know the kindled landskip glows ;
And further, flutter golden showers
On proud Athenai white with towers,
And catching from the murmurous sea,
[Stain'd with deep shadows as of flowers
And dark'ning down to purple bowers
Thro' which the sword-fish darts in glee,]
A strife that cometh not to me.

For in this place of shade and sound,
Hid from the garish heat around,
I feel like one removed from strain
And fever of the happy brain—
Where thoughts thrill fiery into pain:
Like one who, in the pleasant shade
The peaceful pulseless dead have made,
Walking in silence, just perceives
The gaudy world from which he went
Subdue itself to his content,
Like that white globe beyond the leaves!

XIII.

PYGMALION THE SCULPTOR.

"Materiem superabat opus."

1.—IN DEATH'S SHADOW.

UPON the very morn I should have wed
Jove put his silence in a mourning house;
And, coming fresh from feast, I saw her lie
In stainless marriage samite, white and cold,
With orange blossoms in her hair, and gleams
Of the ungiven kisses of the bride
Playing about the edges of her lips.

Then I, Pygmalion, kiss'd her as she slept,
And drew my robe across my face whereon
The haggard revel linger'd dark, and pray'd;

And the sore trouble hollow'd out my heart
To hatred of a harsh unhallow'd youth
As I glode forth. Next, day by day, my soul
Grew conscious of itself and of its fief
Within the shadow of her grave: therewith,
Waken'd a thirst for silence such as dwells
Under the ribs of death: whence slowly grew
Old instincts that had trancëd me to tears
In mine unsinew'd boyhood, precious dreams
That swing like censers spilling balmy oils
O'er poppy flowers of sleep, mild sympathies
Full of faint odours and of music faint
Like buds of roses blowing;—till I felt
Her voice come down from heaven on my soul,
And stir it as a wind that droppeth down
Unseen, unfelt, unheard, until its breath
Troubles the shadows in a sleeping lake.

And the voice said, "Pygmalion," and "Behold,"
I answer'd "I am here;" when thus the voice:
"Put men behind thee—take thy tools, and choose
A rock of marble white as is a star,

Cleanse it and make it pure, and fashion it
After mine image: heal thyself: from grief
Comes glory, like a rainbow from a cloud.
For surely life and death, which dwell apart
In grosser human sense, conspire to make
The breathless beauty and eternal joy
Of sculptur'd shapes in stone. Wherefore thy life
Shall purify itself and heal itself
In the long toil of love made meek by tears;
And at the last, I shall become again
A part of thee, a beauteous silentness
With speech nor motion, but with influence
Like the dumb glory of the moon: a bliss
Wherein the spirit of our love shall grow
Eternal; and the loss will be redeem'd."

I barr'd the entrance-door to this my tower
Against the hungry world, I hid above
The mastiff-murmur of the town, I pray'd
In my pale chamber. Then I wrought, and chose
A rock of marble white as is a star,
And to her silent image fashion'd clay,

And purified myself and heal'd myself
In the long toil of love made meek by tears.

2.—THE MARBLE LIFE.

The multitudinous light oppress'd me not,
But smiled subdued, as a young mother smiles,
When fearful lest the sunbeam of the smile
Trouble the eyelids of the babe asleep.

As Ocean murmurs when the storm is past
And keeps the echoed thunders many days,
My solitude was troublous for a time
With the new sorrow, and I utter'd doubt
Out of a bitter heart. Yea, oftentimes
I swam from dream to dream and gazed thro' tears
On the weak hands dropt nerveless on my knees.
So held I solemn tryst with Memory—
Who, with the pale babe Hope upon her breast,
Sits haggard, hooded, underneath blue night,
Looking on heaven and seeking evermore
To call to mind her former dwelling-place,

Where Hope was born, beyond the silent stars.
Wherefore I should have harden'd; but the clay
Grew to my touch, and brighten'd, and assumed
Fantastic images of natural things,
Which, melting as the fleecy vapours melt
Around the shining cestus of the moon,
Made promise of the special shape I loved.
Withdrawing back, I gazed. The unshaped stone
Took outline in the dusk, as rocks unhewn
Seen from afar thro' floating mountain mists
Gather strange forms and human lineaments.
And thus mine eye was fill'd with what I sought
As with a naked image, thus I grew
Self-credulous of the form the stone would wear,
And creeping close I strove to fashion clay
After the vision. Day and night, I drew
New comfort from my grief; my tears became
As honey'd rain that makes the woodbine sweet,
Until my task assumed a precious strength
Wherewith I fortified mine inner ear
Against the pleadings of the popular tongue
That babbled at my door; and when there dawn'd

A hand as pure as milk and cold as snow,
A small white hand, a little lady hand,
That peep'd out perfect from the changing mass,
And seem'd a portion of some perfect shape
Unfreed, imprison'd in the stone,—I wept
Warm tears of utter joy, and kiss'd the hand,
As sweet girl-mothers kiss the newly born,
Weak as a mother. Then I heard no more
The murmurous swarm beneath me, women and men;
But, hoarded in my toil, I counted not
The interchanges of the days and nights,
The coming and the going of the sun:
Save when I swoon'd to sleep before the stone,
And dream'd, and dreaming saw the perfect shape
Emblazon'd, like the rainbow in a stream,
On the transparent tapestry of sleep.

Ah me, the joy, the glory, and the dream,
When like a living wonder senseless stone
Smiles to the beating of a heart that hangs
Suspended in the tumult of the blood!
To the warm touch of my creating hand

The marble was as snow; and like the snow
Whereon the molten sunshine gleams as blood,
It soften'd, glow'd, and changed. As one who stands
Beneath the cool and rustling dark to watch
The shadow of his silently beloved
Cross o'er the lighted cottage blind and feel
The brightness of the face he cannot see,
So stood I, trembling, while the shape unborn
Darken'd across the white and milky mass
And left the impress of its loveliness
To guide my constant hand. Slowly my soul
Arose, full-statured, to behold its bourne,
But hoarding up its beauty, ruby-like
Grew fierier burning inward to the core.
Nature herself is not more prodigal
Of her strange pageantry of shapely stars,
Blue meteors, rainbow-woven waters, peaks
Of sunset burning down to golden streets
Of flusht cloud-cities crumbling into night,
Or that weird intermingling of the winds
Wherein the stars show pallid and the clouds
Are churn'd to vapour and thin silvery gleams,—

Than that anointed presence unto which
I bent the sunless stone. For, as I wrought,
The Past came back upon me, like the ghost
Of the To-Come. Whate'er was pure and white,
Soft-shining with a snow-like chastity,
Whate'er was troublous with strange impulses
Such as conduct the cold ooze-dropping tide
To creep into the Morn's pale lap and sob
For awe of that dumb glory, came to me
From youth, from childhood, and from that dim land
Which lies behind the horizon of the sense,
Felt though forgotten : vanishings divine
Of the strange vapours many-shaped and fair
Which moisten sunrise when the eye of heaven
Openeth dimly from the underworld :
Faint instincts of the helpless babe that smiles
At the sweet pictures in its mother's eyes
And lieth with a halo round its head
Of beauty uncompleted : memories
Of young Love's vivid heaven-enthronëd light,
By whose moist rays the pensive soul of youth
Was troubled at the fountains, like a well

Wherein the mirror'd motion of a star
Lies dewy and deep ;—and, amid all, there dwelt
A vaguer glory, deeper sense of power,
Scarce conscious of itself yet ruling all,
Like the hid heart which rocks the jaded blood,
Brightens the cheek, throbs music to the brain,
Yet dwells within the breast scarce recognised,
Save when our pulses warn us and in fear
We pause to listen.—Even so at times
Those visions tranced me to a dumb dismay,
And, sudden music thronging in mine ears,
I hearken'd for that central loveliness
Whose magic guided and created all.

Then languor balmier than the blood i' the veins
When youth and maiden mingle and the moon
Breathes on the odorous room wherein they lie
Chamber'd as in a folded rose's leaves,
Oppress'd me, and a lover's rapture fill'd
My soul to swooning. Lo, I kiss'd the stone,
And toy'd with the cold hand, and look'd for light
In the dim onward-looking marble eyes,

And smooth'd the hair until it seem'd to grow
Soft as the living ringlets tingling warm
Against a heaving bosom. At her feet
I knelt, and tingled to the finger-tips
To gaze upon her breathless loveliness—
Like one who, shuddering, gazes on a shrine
From human eyes kept holy.

Then at last,
Fair-statured, noble, like an awful thing
Frozen upon the very verge of life,
And looking back along eternity
With rayless eyes that keep the shadow Time,
She rose before me in the milky stone,
White-limb'd, immortal ; and I gazed and gazed
Like one that sees a vision, and in awe
Half hides his face, yet looks, and seems to dream.

3.—A VOICE IN HEAVEN SINGS.

Lo, now, in the motionless stone
  Life and Death are united for ever!
Lo, Glory encircles the stone,
The Soul gives a speech of its own
  To the beauty that perishes never.
From the furthest fringe of the night,
  Yearning to thee,
Drawn down to the range of thy light,
  I, Psyche, the Soul, can see!

4.—THE SIN.

Blue night. I threw the lattice open wide,
Drinking the odorous air; and from my height
I saw the watch-fires of the town and heard
The gradual dying of the murmurous day.
Then, as the twilight deepen'd, on her limbs
The silver lances of the stars and moon
Were shatter'd, and the shining fragments fell
Like jewels at her feet. The Cyprian star
Quiver'd to liquid emerald where it hung

On the rib'd ledges of the darkening hills,
Gazing upon her; and, as in a dream,
Methought the marble, underneath that look,
Stirr'd—like a bank of milky asphodels
Kiss'd into tumult by a wind of light.

Whereat there swam upon me utterly
A drowsy sense wherein my holy dream
Was melted, as a pearl in wine: bright-eyed,
Keen, haggard, passionate, with languid thrills
Of insolent unrest, I watch'd the stone,
And lo, I loved it: not as men love fame,
Not as the warrior loves his laurel wreath,
But with prelusion of a passionate joy
That threw me from the height whereon I stood
To grasp at Glory, and with impiousness
Of sweet communing with some living Soul
Chamber'd in that cold bosom. As I gazed,
There was a buzz of revel in mine ears,
And tinkling fragments of a ditty of love,
Warbled by wantons over wine-cups, swam
Like bees within the brain.—Then I was shamed

By her pale beauty, and I scorn'd myself,
And standing at the lattice dark and cool
Watch'd the dim winds of twilight enter in,
And draw a veil about that loveliness
White, dim, and breathed on by the common air.

But, like a snake's moist eye, the dewy star
Of lovers drew me; and I watch'd it grow
Large, soft, and tremulous; and as I gazed
In fascinated impotence of heart,
I pray'd the lifeless silence might assume
A palpable life, and soften into flesh,
And be a beautiful and human joy
To crown my love withal; and thrice the prayer
Blacken'd across my pale face with no word.
But thro' the woolly silver of a cloud
The cool star dripping emerald from the baths
Of Ocean brighten'd in upon my tower,
And touch'd the marble forehead with a gleam
Soft, green, and dewy; and I said "the prayer
Is heard!"
The live-long night, the breathless night,

I waited in a darkness, in a dream,
Watching the snowy figure faintly seen,
And ofttimes shuddering when I seem'd to see
Life, like a taper burning in a scull,
Gleam thro' the rayless eyes : yea, wearily
I hearken'd thro' the dark and seem'd to hear
The low warm billowing of a living breast,
Or the slow motion of anointed limbs
New-stirring into life ; and, shuddering,
Fearing the thing I hoped for, awful eyed,
On her cold breast I placed a hand as cold
And sought a fluttering heart.—But all was still,
And chill, and breathless ; and she gazed right on
With rayless orbs, nor marvell'd at my touch :
White, silent, pure, ineffable, a shape
Rebuking human hope, a deathless thing,
Sharing the wonder of the Sun who sends
His long bright look thro' all futurity.

When Shame lay heavy on me, and I hid
My face, and almost hated her, my work,
Because she was so fair, so human fair,

Yea not divinely fair as that pure face
Which, when mine hour of loss and travail came,
Haunted me, out of heaven. Then the Dawn
Stared in upon her: when I open'd eyes,
And saw the gradual Dawn encrimson her
Like blood that blush'd within her,—and behold
She trembled—and I shriek'd!

With haggard eyes,
I gazed on her, my fame, my work, my love!
Red sunrise mingled with the first bright flush
Of palpable life—she trembled, stirr'd, and sigh'd—
And the dim blankness of her stony eyes
Melted to azure. Then, by slow degrees,
She tingled with the milky warmth of blood:
Her eyes were vacant of a seeing soul,
But dewily the bosom rose and fell,
The lips caught sunrise, parting, and the breath
Fainted thro' pearly teeth.

I was as one
Who gazes on a goddess serpent-eyed,
And cannot fly, and knows to look is death.
O apparition of my work and wish!

The weight of awe oppress'd me, and the air
Swung as the Seas swing around drowning men.

5.—DEATH IN LIFE.

About her brow the marble hair had clung
With wavy tresses, in a simple knot
Bound up and braided; but behold, her eyes
Droop'd downward, as she wonder'd at herself,
Then flush'd to see her naked loveliness,
And trembled, stooping downward; and the hair
Unloosening fell, and brighten'd as it fell,
Till gleaming ringlets tingled to the knees
Veiling her nakedness like golden rain,
And cluster'd round about her where she stood
As yellow leaves around a lily's bud,
Making a fountain round her such as clips
A Naiad in the sunshine, pouring down
And throwing moving shadows o'er the floor
Whereon she stood and brighten'd.

Wondering eyed,

With softly heaving breast and outstretch'd arms,

Slow as an eyeless man who gropes his way,
She thrust a curving foot and touch'd the ground,
And stirr'd; and, downcast-lidded, saw not me.
Then as the foot descended with no sound,
The whole live blood grew pink within the veins
For joy of its own motion. Step by step,
She paced the chamber, groping till she gain'd
One sunlight-slip that thro' the curtain'd pane
Crept slant—a gleaming line on roof and floor;
And there, in light, she pausing sunn'd herself
With half-closed eyes; while flying gleams of gold
Sparkled like flies of fire among her hair,
And the live blood show'd brightlier, as wine
Gleams thro' a curd-white cup of porcelain.

There, stirring not, she paused and sunn'd herself,
With drooping eyelids that grew moist and warm,
What time, withdrawn into the further dark,
I watch'd her, nerveless, as a murderer stretch'd
Under a nightmare of the murder'd man.
And still she, downcast-lidded, saw me not;
But gather'd glory while she sunn'd herself,

Drawing deep breath of gladness such as earth
Breathes dewily in the sunrise after rain.

Then pray'd I, lifting up my voice aloud.
"O apparition of my work and wish!
Thou most divinely fair as she whose face
Haunted me, out of heaven! Raise thine eyes!
Live, love, as thou and I have lived and loved!
Behold me—it is I—Pygmalion.
Speak, Psyche, with thy human eyes and lips,
Speak, to Pygmalion, with thy human soul!"

And still she, downcast-lidded, saw me not,
But gather'd glory as she sunn'd herself.
Yet listen'd murmuring inarticulate speech,
Listen'd with ear inclined and fluttering lids,
As one who lying on a bed of flowers
Hearkeneth to the distant fall of waves,
That cometh muffled in the drowsy hum
Of bees pavilion'd among roses'-leaves
Near to the ears that listen. So she stood
And listen'd to my voice, framing her lips

After the speech; nay, when the sound had ceased,
Still listen'd, with a shadow on her cheek—
Like the Soul's Music, when the Soul has fled,
Fading upon a dead Musician's face.

But, stooping in mine awe, with outstretch'd arms,
I crept to her; nor stirr'd she, till my breath
Was warm upon her neck: then raised she eyes
Of dewy azure, ring in ring of blue
Less'ning in passionate orbs whereon my face
Fell white with yearning wonder; when a cry
Tore her soft lips apart, the gleaming orbs
Widen'd to silvery terror, and she fled,
With locks that shone and arms that waved like foam,
And in the further darkness cower'd and moan'd,
Dumb as a ringdove that with fluttering wings
Watches an adder in the act to leap.

What follow'd was a strange and wondrous dream
Wherein, half conscious, wearily and long
I wooed away her fears with gentle words,
Smooth gestures, and sweet smiles,—with kindness such

As smoothes the terror of a new-yean'd lamb,
So pure, it fears its shadow on the grass;
And all the while thick pulses of my heart
Throng'd hot in ears and eyelids,—for my Soul
Seem'd swooning, deaden'd in the sense, like one
Who sinks in snows, and sleeps, and wakes no more.

Yet was I conscious of a hollow void,
A yearning in the tumult of the blood,
Her presence fill'd not, quell'd not; and I search'd
Her eyes for meanings that they harbour'd not,
Her face for beauty that disturb'd it not.
'Twas Psyche's face, and yet 'twas not her face,
A face most fair, yet not so heavenly fair,
As hers who, when my time of travail came,
Haunted me, out of heaven. For its smile
Brought no good news from realms beyond the sun,
The lips framed heavenly nor human speech,
And to the glorious windows of the eyes
No Soul clomb up—to look upon the stars,
And search the void for glimpses of the peaks
Of that far land of morning whence it comes.

Then, further, I was conscious that my face
Had lull'd her fears; that close to me she came
Tamer than beast, and toy'd with my great beard,
And murmur'd sounds like prattled infants' speech,
And yielding to my kisses kissed again.
Whereat, in scorn of my pale Soul, I cried,
"Here will I feast in honour of this night!"
And spread the board with meats and bread and wine,
And drew the curtain with a wave of arm
Bidding the sunlight welcome: lastly, snatch'd
A purple robe of richness from the wall,
And flung it o'er her while she kiss'd and smiled,
Girdling the waist with clasp and cord of gold.

Then sat we, side by side. She, queenly stoled,
Amid the gleaming fountain of her hair,
With liquid azure orbs and rosy lips
Gorgeous with honey'd kisses; I, like a man
Who loves fair eyes and knows they are a fiend's,
And in them sees a heav'n he knows is hell.
For, like a glorious beast, she ate and drank,
Staining her lips in crimson wine, and laugh'd

To feel the vinous bubbles froth and burst
In veins whose sparkling blood was meet to be
An angel's habitation. Cup on cup
I drain'd in fulness—careless as a god—
A haggard bearded head upon a breast
In tumult like a sun-kist bed of flowers.

But ere, suffused with light, the eyes of Heaven
Widen'd to gaze upon the white-arm'd Moon,
Stiller than stone we reign'd there, side by side.
Yea, like a lonely King whose Glory sits
Beside him,—impotent of life but fair,
Brightly apparelëd but vacant-eyed,
And haunts him with the mockery his woe
Casts o'er its jewel'd brows,—I sat above
The tumult of the town, as on a throne,
Watching her wearily; while far away
Vacant eternity was sown with stars,
And sunset dark'd like dying eyes that shut
Under the waving of an angel's wing.

6.—A VOICE IN HEAVEN SINGS.

1.

From the furthest fringe of the night,
While the arms of the flesh enfold thee,
From the darkening fringe of the night
Whence the Moon is withdrawing her light,
I, Psyche the Soul, behold thee!
The glory is faded, is faded,
Pygmalion!
In the sense is my silence degraded,
And my semblance on earth is gone!

2.

O thou, who couldst symbol in stone,
By strength and endurance unbroken,
The Eternal,—conferring on stone
The yearning and love of thine own
Soul, as a hope and a token!
There cometh a bitter to-morrow,
Weak Heart, weak Heart,
For, far from the range of thy sorrow,
I, Psyche the Soul, depart!

7.—ICHABOD.

THREE days and nights the vision dwelt with me,
Three days and nights we dozed in dreadful state,
Look'd piteously upon by sun and star;
But the third night there pass'd a homeless sound
Across the city underneath my tower,
And lo! there came a roll of muffled wheels,
A shrieking and a hurrying to and fro
Beneath, and I gazed forth. Then far below
I heard the people shriek "A pestilence!"
But, while they shriek'd, they carried forth their Dead,
And flung them out upon the common ways,
And moaning fled: while far across the hills
A dark and brazen sunset ribb'd with black
Glared, like the sullen eyeballs of the plague.

I turn'd to her, the partner of my height:
She, with bright eyeballs sick with wine, and hair
Gleaming in sunset, on a couch asleep.
And lo! a horror lifted up my scalp,

The pulses plunged upon the heart, and fear
Froze my wide eyelids. Peacefully she lay
In purple stole array'd, one little hand
Bruising the downy cheek, the other still
Clutching the dripping goblet, and the light,
With gleams of crimson on the ruinous hair,
Spangling a blue-vein'd bosom whence the robe
Fell back in rifled folds; but dreadful change
Grew pale and hideous on the waxen face,
And in her sleep she did not stir, nor dream.
Therefore, it seem'd, Death pluck'd me by the sleeve,
And, sweeping past, with lean forefinger touch'd
The sleeper's brow and smiled; when, shrinking back,
I turn'd my face away, and saw afar
The brazen sullen sunset ribb'd with black
Glare on her, like the eyeballs of the plague.

O apparition of my work and wish!
Shrieking I fled, my robe across my face,
And left my glory and my woe behind,
And sped, thro' pathless woods, o'er moonlit peaks,
Toward sunrise;—nor have halted since that hour,—

But wander far away, a homeless man,
Prophetic, orphan'd both of name and fame.
Nay, like a timid Phantom evermore
I come and go with haggard warning eyes ;
And some, that sit with lemans over wine,
Or dally idly with the glorious hour,
Turn cynic eyes away and smile aside ;
And some are saved because they see me pass,
And, shuddering, yet constant to their task,
Look up for comfort to the silent stars.

XIV.

ANTONY IN ARMS.

Lo, we are side by side!—One dark arm furls
  Around me like a serpent warm and bare;
The other, lifted 'mid a gleam of pearls,
  Holds a full golden goblet in the air:
Her face is shining through her cloudy curls
  With light that makes me drunken unaware,
And with my chin upon my breast I smile
Upon her, darkening inward all the while.

And thro' the chamber curtains, backward roll'd
  By spicy winds that fan my fever'd head,
I see a sandy flat slope yellow as gold
  To the brown banks of Nilus wrinkling red

In the slow sunset; and mine eyes behold
  The West, low down beyond the river's bed,
Grow sullen, ribb'd with many a brazen bar,
Under the white smile of the Cyprian star.

A bitter Roman vision floateth black
  Before me, in my dizzy soul's despite;
The Roman armour brindles on my back,
  My swelling nostrils drink the fumes of fight:
But then, she smiles upon me!—and I lack
  The warrior will that frowns on lewd delight,
And, passionately proud and desolate,
I smile an answer to the joy I hate.

Joy coming uninvoked, asleep, awake,
  Makes sunshine on the grave of buried powers;
Ofttimes I wholly loathe her for the sake
  Of manhood slipt away in easeful hours:
But from her lips mild words and kisses break,
  Till I am like a ruin mock'd with flowers;
I think of Honour's face—then turn to hers—
Dark, like the splendid shame that she confers.

Lo, how her dark arm holds me!—I am bound
By the soft touch of fingers light as leaves:
I drag my face aside, but at the sound
Of her low voice I turn—and she perceives
The cloud of Rome upon my face, and round
My neck she twines her odorous arms and grieves,
Shedding upon a heart as soft as they
Tears 'tis a hero's task to kiss away!

And then she loosens from me, trembling still
Like a bright throbbing robe, and bids me "go!"—
When pearly tears her drooping eyelids fill,
And her swart beauty whitens into snow;
And lost to use of life and hope and will,
I gaze upon her with a warrior's woe,
And turn, and watch her sidelong in annoy—
Then snatch her to me, flush'd with shame and joy!

Once more, O Rome! I would be son of thine—
This constant prayer my chain'd soul ever saith—
I thirst for honourable end—I pine
Not thus to kiss away my mortal breath.

But comfort such as this may not be mine—
  I cannot even die a Roman death:
I seek a Roman's grave, a Roman's rest—
But, dying, I would die upon her breast!

XV.

FINE WEATHER ON THE DIGENTIA.

HORACE LOQUITUR.

1.

FAVONUS changes with sunny kisses
  The spring's ice-fetters to bands of flowers,
And the delicate Graces, those thin-skin'd Misses,
  Are beginning to dance with the rosy Hours;
The Dryades, feeling the breeze on their bosoms,
Thro' tuby branches are blowing out blossoms;
The naked Naiad of every pool,
Lest the sunshine should drive her to playing the fool,
Lies full length in the water and keeps herself cool;
Pan is piping afar, 'mid the trees,
His ditty dies on the dying breeze,

And, with mouth and eyes
Oped in pretty surprise,
A wood-nymph is leaning her head on his knees,
In a dream, in a dream, with her wild eyes glistening,
Her bosom throbbing, her whole soul listening!
In fact, 'tis the season of billing and cooing,
Amorous flying and fond pursuing,
Kissing, and pressing, and mischief-doing;
And pleasant it is to take one's tipple
In the mild warm breath of the spicy South,
And deftly to fasten one's lips to the mouth
Of a flasket warmer than Venus' nipple!
Pleasant, pleasant, at this the season
When folly is reason and reason treason,
When nought is so powerful near or far
As the palpitating
Titillating
Twinkle, twinkle, twinkle of the Cyprian star!

2.

But what has a shaky quaky fellow,
Full of the sunshine but over-mellow,

To do with the beautiful Lesbian Queen,
The pink-eyed precious with locks of yellow,
The goddess of twenty and sweet eighteen,
Whose double conquest o'er Pride and Spleen
In the Greek King's bed put a viper green
And darken'd the seas with the Grecian force?
Nothing, of course!
Well, even I have of joy my measure
And can welcome the newborn Adonis with pleasure;
For since at Actium, worst of scrapes,
I saved my skin for the good of the nation,
And made my pious asseveration
To scorn ambition and cultivate grapes,
I've found by a curious convolution
Of physical ailments and heavenly stars,
And of wisdom wean'd on the blood-milk of Mars,
That my pluck is surpass'd by my elocution—
And learnt, in fine,
That rosy wine
And sunshine agree with my constitution! (*Bibit.*)

3.

Pleasant it is, I say, to sit here,
  Just in the sunshine without the threshold,
  And, with fond fingers and lips, caress old
Bacchus' bottle, the source of wit, here!
Drowsily hum the honey-bees,
Drowsily murmur the birds in the trees,
Drowsily drops the spicy breeze,
Drowsily I sit at mine ease.
Ye gods! shall I groan at the happy and young about?
Forsake this cool seat with acanthus-flowers hung about?
Go, adder-like, thrusting a venomous tongue about?
  Though old, rather old, and as round as a tun,
  I envy no cupids their frolic and fun;
For while, to the boys and the girls I have sung about,
Venus exhibits her airs and graces,
Her coy coqueting and fond grimaces,
And (at the best of it) brief embraces,
I, without circling her natural boddice,
  I, who am corpulent, even ugly,
  Can loll in the sunshine, sipping snugly
The very milk of the amorous goddess! (*Bibit.*)

4.

An idle life is the life for me,—
Idleness spiced by philosophy!
I care not a fig for the cares of business,
Politics fill me with doubt and dizziness,
Pomps and triumphs are simply a bore to me,
Crude ambition will come no more to me,
I hate the vulgar popular cattle,
And I modestly blush at the mention of battle.
No!—Here is my humble definition
Of a perfectly happy and virtuous condition:
A few fat acres aroundabout,
To give one a sense of possession; a few
Servants to pour the sweet Massic out;
Plenty to eat and nothing to do;
A feeling of cozy and proud virility;
A few stray pence;—
And the tiniest sense
Of self-conserving responsibility!

5

For, what is Life?—or, rather ask here,

What is that fountain of music and motion
We call the Soul?—As I sit and bask here,
I confess that I haven't the slightest notion.
Yet Plato calls it eternal, telling
How its original lofty dwelling
Was among the stars, till, fairly repining
At eternally turning a pivot and shining,
Heaven it quitted
To dwell unpitied
In a fleshly mansion of wining and whining;
Aristotle, I don't know why,
Believes that, born up above in the sky
The moment that Body is born on the earth,
'Tis married to Body that moment of birth;
Hippo and others, whose heads were a muddle,
Affirm 'tis compounded of water—puddle!
Fire, not a few, with Democritus, swear;
While others—chameleons—reduce it to Air;
Water and fire, cries Hippocrates!
No, water and earth, cries Xenophanes!
Earth and fire, cries Parmenides!
Stop! cries Empedocles,—all of these!

Ennius follow'd Pythagoras, thinking
The transmigration of spirits a truth ;—
A doctrine I choose to apply in sooth
To the spirit that lies in the wine I'm drinking ;
But, what to an egotist even seems odd, he
Swore Homer survived in his (Ennius') body.
Speculation, muddle, trouble,
Some see obliquely, others double,
While under their noses,
Which smell not the roses,
Truth placidly bursts like a spangled bubble.

6.

Altogether, they puzzle me quite,
They all seem wrong and they all seem right,
And we know as much of the Soul just now
As if none of the sages had kick'd up a row.
Its nature remains an unsatisfied question ;
But Epicurus has flatly tried
To prove that the Soul is closely allied
To wine, and sunshine, and good digestion.
For without any prosing, head-racking, or preaching,

That's the construction I put on his teaching!
'Tis simple: the Soul and the Body are one,
Like the Sun itself and the light of the Sun,
Born to change with all other creations,
Homunculi, qualities, emanations,
To pass thro' wondrous and strange gradations;
And if this be the case, our best resource
Is to make the most of our time, of course,
Nor grumble and question till hoary and hoarse.
And I slightly improve upon Epicurus,
Who shirk'd good living, as some assure us,
And assert, from experience long and rare,
That body and soul can be perfectly snug,
With sunshine, fresh air,
And no physical care,
In a garden that never requires to be dug.

7.

I, Quintus Horatius Flaccus, am learning
From the tuneful stars in my zenith turning,
From yonder sunshine, from earth's fat blessing,
From the oily juice my old liver caressing,

From my bachelorhood, which is wide awake,
 That the sum of good is a life of ease,
 A friend or two, if the humour please,
And not a tie it would pain you to break.
Call me selfish, indolent, vain,
But I don't and won't see the virtue of pain,
Be it of body or be it of brain;
Call me grovelling, earthly, mean,
But I've a philosophy void of spleen;
I hate to be cold, and I like to be warm,
 Just for his sunshine I worship Apollo,
 And my soberest virtue resembles the swallow,
Flying close to the ground—to avoid the storm.
Actium finish'd my education,
For it taught me the doctrine of self-preservation.
I hate the barking of Scylla's dogs,
 Round Charybdis your sailor may spin, but not I:—
 In short, I am one of those excellent hogs
That grunt in the Grecian epicure's sty.
Day by day, my delight has grown wider
 Since I learnt that wine is a natural good,
 And the stubborn donkey called Fortitude

Has a knack of upsetting the bile of its rider.
All creeds that bore one are mere vexation ;
But I firmly believe, and no man dare doubt me,
In Massia taken in moderation,
And I like to dwell where no fools can flout me—
Sans physical care,
In the sunny air,
And to sing—when I feel the fresh world about me!

(*Bibit.*)

8.

Bear witness, Flower!—One's sense perceives
The rich sap lying within your leaves,
Which lusciously swoon to a soft blood-red
As the sunlight woos them from overhead!
Now, here is a parallel worth inspection
Of body and blood in perfect connexion
With what some call Soul, that obscure abstraction
Which I have proved to my satisfaction
To be body in lesser or greater perfection.
The perfect parts of the perfect flower
Were nourish'd by sunshine for many an hour,
Till the sunshine within them o'erflowing,—hence

The juice whose odorous quintessence,
Though sweetly expressing the parts and the whole,
Is simply a part of the whole, and still
Inseparate from the general will.
The Flower is the Body, the Scent is the Soul!
See! I press a thorn in the milky stalk:
The small thing droops o'er the garden walk,
The soft leaves shiver, the sap runs dry,
And never more will the flower's mild eye
Drink the breath of the moon—it will linger, and die.
But the scent of the flower, some would cry, is the sweeter;
  True, but the scent, every moment, grows less,
  And, further observing, they would confess,
That the flower, as a flower, is the incompleter!
  Well, between my fingers I sharply press
The delicate leaves, and thro' every vein
The perfect anatomy shrinks with pain,
  And the flower with its odorous quintessence
Will never, 'tis clear, be perfection again.
  Bah! I pluck it, I pluck it, and cast it hence,
As Death plucks humanity body and brain.

But the odour has not yet flown, you cry,
It sweetens the air, tho' the flower doth die!
Of course; and the feelers and stem and leaves,
And the sap and the odour it interweaves,
No longer perfect and gastronomic,
Are in common resolving themselves, one perceives,
Back to first principles—say atomic;
And whatever destination your fine
Hard-headed philosophers choose to assign
To the several parts, they are reft of their power,
And, so far as concerns its true functions—to scent
The soft air, and look fair—and its first sweet intent,
'Tis clear that the whole is no longer a Flower.

9.

Take that bulky and truly delectable whole,
The egotistic disciple of Bacchus,
With small hare's-eyes and gray hairs on his poll,
Myself—good Quintus Horatius Flaccus!
There's a Body! There's a Soul!
All smooth and round, some indifferent parts,
Sound head, rich blood, and the gayest of hearts,

Forming a total whose conservation
Is the subject of constant deliberation
To the most important head in the nation!
Mortal, you see! and a writer of rhyme!
But in spite of approaching annihilation,
He makes the very best use of his time:
Sips Massic, lives lightly in innocent sort,
Avoids all bother which cuts life short,
And is conscious how soon from this state he must sever,
To dissolve his parts into dust for ever.
Many a year, over Rome's dominions,
Has he vaunted his epicurean opinions;
He may be wrong, he may be right,
So he roars his creed in no mad heroics,—
Since down in the grave, where all creeds unite,
Even Epicureans are changed to Stoics. *(Bibit.)*

10.

Humph, the grave!—not the pleasantest prospect, affirms
This quiet old heart starting up with a beat—
Well, 'tis rather hard that liquor so sweet

Goes simply to flavour a meal for worms!
After all, I'm a sensible man,
To render my span
As happy and easeful as ever I can.
To-morrow may mingle, who knows, who knows,
  The Life that is Dream with the Death that is Sleep,
And the grass that covers my last repose
  May make a sward where the lambkins leap
Round a mild-eyed mellifluous musical boy
Who pipes to his flock in a pastoral joy,
While the sun that is shining upon him there
Draws silver threads thro' his curly hair,
And Time with long shadows stalks past the spot,
And the Hours pass by, and he sees them not!
Instead of moping and idly rueing it,
Now, this is the pleasantest way of viewing it!—
To think, when all is over and done,
Of insensately feeling one's way to the sun,
Of being a part of the verdure that chases
The mild west-wind into shady places,
While one's liver, warming the roots of a tree,
Creeps upward and flutters delectably

In the leaves that tremble and sigh and sing,
And the breath bubbles up in a daisy ring,
And the heart, mingling strangely with rains and snows,
Bleeds up thro' the turf in the blood of a rose.

11.

Which reminds me, here, that the simile drawn
From the flower that is withering on the lawn,
May, by a stretch of the thought, apply
To the universe—ocean, earth, air, and sky;
And dividing the whole into infinite less,
First principles, atomics numberless,
We find that the sum of the universe strange
Suffers continual mystical change;
While the parts of the whole, tho' their compounds range
Thro' all combinations from men down to daisies,
Are eternal, unchangeable, suffer no phases.
So that Death, to the dullest of heads so unsightly,
Is (here I improve Epicurus slightly)
Is but the period of dissolution
Into some untraceable constitution

Of the several parts of the Body and Soul,—
And a total extinction of Man as a whole.
As to Time—mere abstraction! With even motion,
Like waves that gathering foamy speech
Grow duskily up on a moonlit beach,
And seem to increase the huge bulk of the ocean,
Hours roll upon hours in the measureless sea
        Of eternity:
        Never ceasing, they seem increasing;
But the parts of the Infinite, changing never,
Increase not, tho' changing, the Whole, the For Ever.
Time? Call it a compound, if you please,
A divisible drop in eternal seas,
An abstract figure, by which we men
Try to count our sensations again and again,
And then you will know, perceiving we must
Nourish some compound with dust of dust,
And seeing how short our sensations and powers,
        Why I am one,
        Who sits in the sun,
Whose Time is no limited number of hours,
But wine ever-present, in nectarine showers.

12.

O Mutability, dread abstraction,
Counsel Horatius, thy plump epitome,
How to be wise in the satisfaction
Of his moderate needs in a half-inaction.
Shall I be lachrymose? Not a bit o' me.
While Propertius grows love-sick and weary and wan,
While thou, Virgil, singest of arms and the man,
While assassins on Cæsar sharpen their eyes,
While Agrippa stands grimly on blood-stained decks,
While Maecenas flirts with the female sex,
Teach me to sport and philosophize!
O Mutability, lasting ever,
Changing ever, yet changing never,
Teach me, O teach me, and make me wise!—
In the dreadful depth of thine eyeballs dumb,
Strange meanings flutter and pass to nought,
And beautiful images fade as they come,
Thro' an under-trouble of shady thought!

13.

Yonder, yonder, the River doth run,

From sun to shade, and from shade to sun,
  Shaking the lilies to seed as it flows,
  Under the willow-trees taking a dose,
And waking up in a flutter of fun!
Could you look at the leaves of yonder tree!
The wind is stirring them as the sun is stirring me!
The woolly clouds move quiet and slow,
  In the pale blue calm of the tranquil skies,
And their shades that run on the grass below
  Leave purple dreams in the violet's eyes!
The vine droops over my head with bright
  Clusters of purple and green—the rose
  Breaks her heart on the air—and the orange glows
Like golden lamps in an emerald night.*
While I sit, with the stain of the wine on my lip,
Shall nature and I part fellowship?
No, by Bacchus! This view from the threshold of
    home
Is as glad to the core, and as sorrow-despising,
As Aphroditè when fresh from the foam
That still on her bosoms was falling and rising,

* "Golden lamps in a green night."—ANDREW MARVEL.

While the sunshine crept thro' her briny hair
And mingled itself with the shadows there,
And her deepening eyes drank their azure from air,
And she blushed a new beauty surpassingly fair!

14.

'Tis absurd to tell me to ruffle a feather,
Because there may soon be a change of weather.
When the Dog-Star foams, I will lie in the shade,
And watch the white sun thro' an emerald glade;
When winter murmurs with rain and storm,
I will watch my hearth smile to itself, and keep warm;
And for Death, who having fulfilled his task
  Leaves his deputy Silence in houses of mourning,—
Well, I hope he no troublesome questions will ask,
  But knock me down, like an ox, without warning.
Like the world, I most solemnly promise devotion
To pleasure commingled of light, music, motion.
That kind of pleasure like sunny rain,
Which drowns the shoots of a transient pain,
But sets the seeds deeper in soil of the brain,
Till, stronger and fiercer, they blossom again,

Is as foul as that Fortune whose kisses divert you
  While she opens a vein with a golden knife,
  Or that rigid Morality, plague of my life,
Which thinks one a cushion and thumps one with
      virtue.
But I like (as I said) to sit here in my mirth,
To be part of the joy of the sweet-smelling earth,
To feel the blood blush like a flower with its glee,
To sing like a bird, to be stirr'd like a tree,
Drowsily, drowsily, sit at mine ease,
While the odd rhymes buzz in my brain like bees,
And over my wine-cup to chirp and to nod,
        Ay to sit—till I fall
        Like that peach from the wall—
Self-sufficient, serene, happy-eyed,—like a God!

(*Bibit.*)

15.

Ay, crop the corn with the crooked sickle,
  Sow harvest early and reap too late,
Prove Fortune friendly or false or fickle,
  Blunder and bother with aching pate,
Attempting to conquer chance or fate,

Struggle, speculate, dig, and bleed,
Reap the whirlwind of Venus' seed,
O senseless, impotent human breed!
What avails! what avails! Were ye less intent
  On your raking and digging, perchance ye'd behold
  The fleecy vapours above you roll'd
Round the dozing Deities dead to strife,
With their mild great eyes on each other bent
Enchanging a wisdom indifferent
To the native honours of death and life.
Sober truths of a pleasure divine
Keep them supine!
The grand lazy fellows have nothing to do
With the hubble and trouble of me or of you,
The stars break around them in silver foam,
And they calmly amuse themselves, sometimes, by
    stealing
A peep at us pigmies, with much the same feeling
With which, from the candour and quiet of home,
I glance at the strife of political Rome.
Serene, happy-eyed, self-sufficient, they rest
On the hill where the blue sky is leaning her breast :—

Jove seated supreme in the midst, at his side
  Apollo the Sun and Selene the Moon,
Juno half dozing, her foot of pride
On the neck of Venus the drowsy-eyed,
  And Pallas humming the spheric tune.

16.

Flash!
Lightning, I swear!—there's a tempest brewing!
Crash!
Thunder, too—swift-footed lightning pursuing!
The leaves are troubled, the winds drop dead,
The air grows ruminant overhead—
Splash!
That great round drop fell pat on my nose.
Flash! crash! splash!—
I must run for it, I suppose.
O what a flashing and crashing and splashing,
  The earth is rocking, the skies are riven—
Jove in a passion, in god-like fashion,
  Is breaking the crystal urns of heaven.

XVI.

FINE WEATHER BY BAIAE.

VIRGIL TO HORACE.

1.

SWEET is soft slumber, Horace, after toil,
To him who holds the glebe and ploughs the fruitful soil,
Sweet to salt-blooded mariners, on decks washed red with storm,
Deep sleep wherein past tempest and green waves
Make shadows multiform;

2.

Sweet 'tis to Cæsar, when the red star, grown
Swart with war's dust, doth fade, to loll upon a throne

Dispensing gifts, while on his lips a crafty half-smile
dies,
And the soft whispers of approving Rome
Fan his half-closëd eyes!

3.

Sweet to Tibullus, sick and out of tune,
What time his elegies like wolves howl at the moon,
Comes Pity loos'ning Delia's zone as breezes part a
cloud;
And sweet to thee a wine-cup rough with sleep,
After the tawny crowd.

4.

And further, sweetly comes a scroll from thee
To Virgil where he dwells at Baiae near the sea—
For, sick with servile snakes of state that twine round
Cæsar's foot,
He welcomes thy moist greeting and thy thought
Poetically put.

5.

Such alternation of unrest and rest,
All fitful peace and passion of the yearning breast,
Deepen the meanings flashing swift in Joy's pink-lidded eyne,
And help the Hours to juggle with the fruits
Of easy creeds like thine.

6.

The time-glass runs, the seasons come and go,
After the rain, the flowers, after the flowers, the snow;
This Hour is pale and olive-crown'd, that splash'd with rebel-mud—
This, flusht to gaze on Cæsar's laurell'd brows,
That, drunk with Cæsar's blood!

7.

Shall merest mortal man with drowsy nod
Sit under purple vine and doze and ape the god?
Wave down the everlasting strife of earth and air and sea?
And, like a full-fed fruit that gorges light,
Grow rotten on the tree?

8.

Leave the grand mental war that mortals keep?
Eat the fat ears of corn, yet neither sow nor reap?
Loll in the sunshine, sipping sweets, what time the din
of fights
Quenches the wind round Troy, and very gods
Feel dizzy on their heights?

9.

Nay, friend!—For such a man each hour supplies
Portents that mock his ease, affright his languid eyes:
The very elements are leagued to goad him blood and
brain,
The very Sun sows drouth within his throat
Until it raves for rain!

10.

Methinks I see thee sitting in the sun,
Whose kisses melt thy crusty wrinkles one by one:
Thy lips droop darkly with a worm of thought, half
sad, half wroth,
Which stirs the chrysalis mouth, then, ripe with wine,
Bursts like a golden moth.

11.

Unfaith is with thee, Horace. Sun and wind
Disturb the tranquil currents of thy heart and mind;
In midst of joy, comes pigmy doubt, prick-pricking like a flea,
Till, wide awake, you rack your brains to prove
Your perfect joy to me.

12.

O better far, if Man would climb, to range
Thro' sun and thunder-storm tempestuous paths of change,
To mingle with the motion huge of earth and air and main,
And lastly, fall upon a bed of flowers
When wearied down by pain.

13.

Deep, deep, within Man's elemental parts—
Earth, water, fire, and air that mix in human hearts,—
Subsists Unrest that seeketh Rest, and flashes into gleams

That haunt the soul to action, and by night
Disturb our sleep with dreams.

14.

And thus we fashion with a piteous will
The gods in drowsy mildness seated on a hill,
The day before them evermore, the starry night behind,—
Inheritors of the divine repose
We seek and cannot find.

15.

Woe, woe, to him, who craving that calm boon
Falleth to sleep on beds of poppy flowers too soon!
The elements shall hem him in and fright his shrieking soul,
And, since he asks for light, Lightning itself
Shall scorch his eyes to coal!

16.

My Horace!—I am here beside the deep,
Weaving at will this verse for Memory to keep:

I share the sunshine with my friend, and like a lizard
bask;
But I, friend, doubt this summer joy,—and you
Shall answer what I ask.—

17.

Bluff March has blown his clarion out of tune,
Gone is the blue-edged sickle of the April moon;
Faded hath fretful May behind a tremulous veil of
rain,—
But I would the boisterous season of the winds
And snows were here again!

18.

For I am kneeling on the white sea-sand,
Letting the cold soft waves creep up and kiss my
hand;
A golden glare of sunshine fills the blue air at my
back,
And swims between the meadows and the skies,
Leaving the meadows black.

19.

All is as still and beautiful as sleep :
Nay, all *is* sleep—the quiet air, the azure deep ;
The cool blue waves creep thro' my fingers with a
silver gleam,
As, lost in utter calm, I neither think
Nor act, but only dream.

20.

This is the poetry of Heart's repose,
For which my spirit yearn'd thro' drifting winds and
snows—
Only the tingling coolness on my hand seems part akin
To that bleak winter warring when the dream
Of peace arose within.

21.

What time I dream'd of this, the winds, cast free,
Swoop'd eagle-like and tore the white bowels of the
sea ;
The winter tempest moved above, and storm on storm
did frown ;—

I saw the awful Sea bound up in cloud
And then torn hugely down.

22.

Within my blood arose the wild commotion,
My soul was battling abroad with winds and ocean ;
But in the centre of the wrath, all nature, sea and sky,
Call'd out aloud for peace divine as this,
And lo, I join'd the cry.

23.

And calm has come, and June is on the deep,
The winds are nested, and the earth takes mellow sleep ;
Yet, friend, my soul, though husht in awe, feels peace so still is pain,—
And the monotonous yearning voice within
Calls out for war again !

24.

For hark ! into my dream of golden ease
Breaketh the hollow murmur of untroubled seas ;

And behold, my blood awakens with a thrill and sinks
and swells,
As when low breezes die and rise again
On beds of asphodels.

25.

Ay, now, when all is placid as a star,
My soul in incompleteness longs for active war;
Amid its utter happiness, it sighs imperfectly
In answer to the beautiful unrest
Within the sleeping sea.

26.

Unsatisfied, I hunger on the land,
Only subdued by this bright water on my hand;
The beating heart within my breast for louder
utterance yearns—
I listen, and the sympathetic sea
Its endless moan returns.

27.

Quiet, monotonous, breathless, almost drown'd,
Inaudibly audible, felt scarce heard, cometh the sound,

Monotonous, so monotonous, but oh! so sweet, so sweet,
When my hid heart is throbbing forth a voice,
And the two voices meet.

28.

The void within the calm for which I yearned,
Until this moment was imperfectly discerned;
But now I feel to the roots of life an inner melody,
That harmonises my unquiet heart
With the unquiet sea.

29.

Hear I the crawling movements of the main?
Or hear I dim heart-echoes dying in the brain?
Is there but one impatient moan, and is it of the sea?
And, if two voices speak, which voice belongs
To ocean, which to me?

30.

The sounds have mingled into some faint whole,
Inseparate, trembling o'er the fibres of my soul;

And the cool waves have a magic all my swooning
blood to quell;
The sea glides thro' and thro' me, and my soul
Keeps sea-sound like a shell.

31.

Ah, the monotonous music in my soul,
Enlarging like the waves, murmuring without control!—
Is it that changeful nature can rest not night nor day?
And is the music born of this lorn Man,
Or Ocean,—Horace, say?

32.

Are these vibrations but a prophecy
Of wondrous storms unborn, in nature and in me?
And is this sweetly sad unrest that I and Ocean share
The vital principle abroad in earth
And water, fire and air?

33.

Is there a climbing element in life
Which is at war with rest, alternates strife with strife,

Whereby we reach eternal seas upon whose shores
unstirr'd
Ev'n Joy can sleep,—because no moan like this
Within those waves is heard ?

XVII.

THE VOICE IN THE SNOW.

1.

WE are the fairies of the Snow,
Hushing sweet hearts where'er we go !—
Our gentle motion from the skies
Has voiceless music for the eyes,
And with that music unaware
We stir the grey and wintry air,
And, mirror'd in the eyes, we roll
With thought-like glamour to the Soul!

2.

We are the fairies of the Snow,
Hushing the heart where'er we go !—

We paint the earth in winter hours
With stainless pictures of the flowers,
We kiss the dark earth t' l it grows
A silver cloud of pure repose,
Till nature's troublous yearning sense
Hushes itself to reverence!

3.

We are the fairies of the Snow,
Hushing the heart where'er we go!—
We weave with fleecy fingers sweet
The dying Winter's winding-sheet,
We whisper comfort while we place
Our parting kisses on his face,
And leave upon the face we press
Pale signs of unborn loveliness!

4.

We are the fairies of the Snow,
Working for weal where'er we go!
We warm the quick'ning babe of spring
Under a silken carpeting,

And darkening in fleecy flocks
We seek the roots of trees and rocks—
And blowing hence, in summer hours,
We are the fairies of the Flowers!

XVIII.

METEMPSYCHOSIS.

1.

I DISTINCTLY remember (and who dares doubt me?)
  Having been (now, I care not who believes!)
An ape with a forest around about me—
  Prodigious trees and enormous leaves,
Great bulks of flowers, gigantic grasses,
  Boughs that bent not to any gale:
And thence, I date my contempt for Asses,
  And my deep respect for the Devil's Tail!

2.

I shall never forget the exquisite feeling
  Of elevation, sans thought, sans care,

When I twisted my tail round the wood's bough-
ceiling,
And swung, meditatively, in the air.—
There's an advantage!—Fairer shapes can
Aspire, yearn upward, tremble and glow,
But, by means of their posteriority, apes can
Look down on aspirants that walk below!

3.

There was a life for a calm philosopher,
Self-supplied with jacket, and trousers, and socks,
Nothing to learn, no hopes to get cross over,
A head that resisted the hardest knocks,
Liquor and meat in serene fruition,
A random income from taxes free,
No cares at all, and but one ambition—
To swing by the Tail to the bough of a tree!

4.

Whence I firmly believe, to the consternation
Of puppies who think monkeyosophy sin,

In gradual human degeneration
  And a general apely origin.
Why, the simple truth's in a nutshell or thimble,
  Though it rouses the monkey in ignorant elves;
And the Devil's Tail is a delicate symbol
  Of apehood predominant still in ourselves.

5.

Pure class government, family glory,
  Were the delights of that happy lot;
My politics were serenely Tory,
  And I claim'd old descent from God knows what:
Whence I boast extraction loftier, nobler,
  Than the beggarly Poets one often meets,
A boast I am happy to share with the cobbler
  Who whisked his Tail out—to whip John Keats.

6.

There was a life, I assever! With reasons
  That lead me to scorn every star-gazing Ass;
And because I loved it, at certain seasons
  'Tis a pleasure to gaze in the looking-glass.

When the bright sun beckons the spring, green-deckt,
up,
The Ape swells within me : whenever I see
Mortals look skyward, walking erect up,
I long for a Tail and a large strong Tree !

XIX.

PROTEUS.

1.

Into the living elements of things
  I, Proteus, mingle, seeking strange disguise:
I track the Sun-god on an eagle's wings,
  Or look at horror thro' a murderer's eyes,
In shape of hornëd beast my shadow glides
Among broad-leavëd flowers that blow 'neath Afric tides.

2.

A wind of ancient prophecy swept down,
  And wither'd up my glory—where I lay

On Paris' bosom, in the Trojan town :
  Troy vanish'd ; and I wander'd far away,—
Till, lying on a Virgin's breast, I gazed
  Thro' infant's eyes, and saw, as in a dream,
The great god Pan, whom I had raised and praised,
  Float, huge, unsinew'd, down a mighty stream,
With leaves and lilies heaped about his head
  And a weird music hemming him around,
While, dropping from his nerveless fingers dead,
  A brazen sceptre plunged with hollow sound :
A trackless Ocean wrinkling far away
Open'd its darkness for the unking'd day :
Moreover, as he floateth on, at rest,
  With lips that flutter'd still and seem'd to speak,
An Eagle, swooping down upon his breast,
  Picked his blank eyeballs out with golden beak.

3.

Thro' wondrous change on change—
Haunted for ever by a hollow tune
Made ere the birth of Sun or Stars or Moon—
  I, Proteus, range.

4.

Nay, evermore I grow
Darker, with deeper power to see and know.—
For in the end, I, Proteus, shall cast
All wondrous shapes aside but one alone,
And stand (while roundabout me in the Vast
The Earth, Sun, Stars, and Moon, burn out at last)—
A Skeleton, that kneels before a Throne.

EPILOGUE.

TO MARY ON EARTH.

"*Simplex munditiis!*"

EPILOGUE.

TO MARY ON EARTH.

1.

So! now the task is ended; and to-night,
Sick, impotent, no longer soul-sustain'd,
Withdrawing eyes from that ideal height
Where, in low undertones, those Spirits plain'd,
Each full of special glory unattain'd,—
I turn on you, Sweet-Heart, my weary sight.—
Shut out the darkness, shutting in the light:
So! now the task is ended. What is gain'd?

2.

First, sit beside me. Place your hand in mine.
From deepest fountain of your veins the while

Call up your Soul ; and briefly let it shine
In those grey eyes with mildness feminine.
Yes, smile, Dear !—you are truest when you smile.

3.

My heart to-night is calm as peaceful dreams.—
Afar away the wind is shrill, the culver
Blows up and down the moors with windy gleams,
The birch unlooseneth her locks of silver
And shakes them softly on the mountain streams,
And o'er the grave that holds my David's dust
The Moon uplifts her empty dripping horn :
Thither my fancies turn, but turn in trust,
Not wholly sadly, faithful though forlorn.
For you, too, love him, mourn his life's quick fleeting ;
We think of him in common. Is it so ?—
Your little hand has answer'd, and I know
His name makes music in your heart's soft beating ;
And——well, 'tis something gain'd for him and me—
Him, in his heaven, and me, in this low spot,
Something his eyes will see, and joy to see—
That you, too, love him, though you knew him not.

4.

Yet this is bitter. We were boy and boy,
Hand link'd in hand we dreamt of power and fame,
We shared each other's sorrow, pride, and joy,
To one wild tune our swift blood went and came,
Eyes drank each other's hope with flash of flame.
Then, side by side, we clomb the hill of life,
We ranged thro' mist and mist, thro' storm and strife;
But then,——it is so bitter, now, to feel
That his pale Soul to mine was so akin,
Firm-fix'd on goals we each set forth to win,
So twinly conscious of the sweet Ideal,
So wedded (God forgive me if I sin!)
That neither he, my friend, nor I could steal
One glimpse of heaven's divinities—alone,
And flushing seek his brother, and reveal
Some hope, some joy, some beauty, else unknown;
Nor, bringing down his sunlight from the Sun,
Call sudden up, to light his fellow's face,
A smile as proud, as glad, as that I trace
In your dear eyes, now, when my work is done.

5.

Love gains in giving. What had I to give
Whereof his Poet-Soul was not possest?
What gleams of stars he knew not, fugitive
As lightning-flashes, could I manifest?
What music fainting in a clearer air?
What lights of sunrise from beyond the grave?
What pride in knowledge that he could not share?—
Ay, Mary, it is bitter; for I swear
He took with him, to heav'n, no wealth I gave.

6.

No, Love, it is not bitter! Thoughts like those
Were sin these songs I sing you must adjust.
Not bitter, ah, not bitter!—God is just;
And, seeing our one-knowledge, just God chose,
By one swift stroke, to part us. Far above
The measure of my hope, my pride, my love,
He, like an exhalation, thus arose
Above our seasons, suns and rains and snows,—
Hearing in a diviner atmosphere
Music we only see, when, dewy and dim,

The stars thro' gulfs of azure darkness swim,
Music I seem to see, but cannot hear.
But evermore, my Poet, on his height,
Fills up my Soul with sweetness to the brim,
Rains influence, and warning, and delight;
And *now*, I smile for pride and joy in him!

7.

I said, Love gains by giving. And to know
That I, who could not glorify my Friend,
Soul of my Soul, although I loved him so,
Have power and strength and privilege to lend
Glimpses of heav'n to Thee, of hope, of bliss!
Power to go heavenward, pluck flowers and blend
Their hues in wreaths I give you with a kiss—
You, Love, who climb not up the heights at all!
To think, to think, I never could upcall
On his dead face, so proud a smile as this!

8.

Most just is God: who bids me not be sad
For his dear sake whose name is dear to thee,

Who bids me proudly climb and sometimes see
With joy a glimpse of him in glory clad;
Who, further, bids your life be proud and glad,
When I have climb'd and seen, for joy in me.
My lowly-minded, gentle-hearted Love!
I bring you down his gifts, and am sustain'd:
You watch and pray—I climb—he stands above.
So, now the task is ended, what is gain'd?

9.

This knowledge.—Better in your arms to rest,
Better to love you till my heart should break,
Than pause to ask if he who would be blest
Should love for more than his own loving's sake.
So closer, closer still; for (while afar,
Mile upon mile toward the polar star,
Now in the autumn time our Poet's dust
Sucks back thro' grassy sods the flowers it thrust
To feel the summer on the outer earth)
I turn to you, and on your bosom fall.
Love grows by giving. I have given my all.
So, smile—to show you hold the gift of worth.

10.

Ay, all the thanks that I on earth can render
To him who sends me such good news from God,
Is, in due turn, to thy young life to tender
Hopes that denote, while blossoming in splendour,
Where an invisible Angel's foot hath trode.
So, Sweet-Heart, I have given unto thee,
Not only such poor song as here I twine,
But Hope, Ambition, all of mine or me,
My flesh and blood, and more, my Soul divine.
Take all, take all! Ay, wind white arms about
My neck and from my Soul draw bliss for thine:
Smile, Sweet-Heart, and be happy—lest thou doubt
How much the gift I give thee makes thee mine!

THE END.

CPSIA information can be obtained
at www.ICGtesting.com
Printed in the USA
LVHW040427110522
718423LV00002B/428

9 783375 004507